# Flight
# from the
# U.S.S.R

Library and Archives Canada Cataloguing in Publication

Turašsvili, Dato, 1966-
[Jinsebis t'aoba. English]
        Flight for the USSR / Dato Turashvili.

Translation of: Jinsebis t'aoba.
Issued in print and electronic formats.
ISBN 978-1-77161-156-5 (paperback).--ISBN 978-1-77161-157-2 (html).--
ISBN 978-1-77161-158-9 (pdf)

        I. Title. II. Title: Jinsebis t'aoba. English.

PK9169.T89J5613 2015                899'.9693            C2015-906901-7
                                                         C2015-906902-5

Pubished by Mosaic Press, Oakville, Ontario, Canada, 2015.
Distributed in the United States by Bookmasters (www.bookmasters.com).
Distributed in the U.K. by Gazelle Book Services (www.gazellebookservices.co.uk).

MOSAIC PRESS, Publishers
Copyright © 2008, 2013 Dato Turashvili
Translation Copyright © 2015 Mosaic Press and Maya Kiasashvili

Design and layout by Eric Normann

Published with the support of:
The Georgian National Book Center and
The Ministry of Culture and Monument Protection of Georgia

We acknowledge the financial support of
the Government of Canada through the
Canada Book Fund (CBF) for this project.

Nous reconnaissons l'aide financière du gouvernement du Canada par l'entremise du Fonds du livre du Canada (FLC) pour ce projet.

  Canadian Patrimoine
Heritage canadien

**MOSAIC PRESS**
1252 Speers Road, Units 1 & 2
Oakville, Ontario L6L 5N9
phone: (905) 825-2130

info@mosaic-press.com

# Flight from the U.S.S.R

## Dato Turashvili

Translated by
Maya Kiasashvili

We acknowledge the kind support of:

**GEORGIAN NATIONAL BOOK CENTER**

MINISTRY OF CULTURE
AND MONUMENT PROTECTION
OF GEORGIA

# CONTENTS

These blue days and this sunshine of childhood...

# PREFACE

I didn't mean to publish this book. I naively believed that after the disintegration of the USSR, Georgia's Soviet past would become a bitter memory. I was wrong. It turned out that the past can come back with a vengeance, especially if we can't leave it behind.

We may have distanced ourselves from that country and those times, but we have failed to alter the mindset acquired while we were part of what was called the 'Empire of Evil,' when benevolence was scarce. A superpower that made groundbreaking advances during the 'Space Race,' could not manage to produce a simple pair of jeans. What can be more innocent than a pair of jeans? So if they couldn't produce them, they just banned them.

These banned jeans became sweeter than forbidden fruit. Soviet youth were determined to get them at all costs and, not surprisingly, smuggling boomed. Occasionally, there

would be a pair of genuine US jeans among those smuggled
from all over the world. In those days, every pair of jeans
was believed to be American and, as Soviet propaganda was
particularly set on destroying American values, many of us
thought that happiness lay where jeans were abundant.

There was a grain of truth in such a belief because
the Soviet state denied its citizens basic civil rights, the
right of property among them. Freedom only came when
you reached your grave, or at least the authorities stopped
worrying about your freedom when you were safely six feet
under. Even atheistic officials knew that sooner or later
they would be laid to rest in the same ground, so no one
was denied the right to a grave.

There might have been other reasons, but the fact was
that a grave was the only property people owned. Such
political attitudes marked the start of change in Georgians'
taste for the worst. For centuries, traditional Georgian
graveyards were simple and modest. Then in the Soviet era,
graves became extremely elaborate—adorned with marble
tables and benches, statues, bikes and even cars. Soviet
Georgians were confident in only one thing—their graves
belonged to them. So they were taken care of and zealously
protected. People built and decorated them as they would
do if they owned real estate. The authorities turned a blind
eye to graveyard eccentricities. The principles of the Soviet
regime did not extend to the Georgian graveyards.

The Georgian authorities demonstrated more respect to
the dead than to the living. However, there was one pre-
requisite for a guaranteed grave—you had to die a natural
death. If you were executed for a crime, a dead convict would
certainly be buried but without a proper grave. Starting
in the 1920s, thousands of executed convicts found their
eternal resting place in various unmarked stretches of land
across the country. Very often, even the diggers assigned

the job of preparing a deep hole (not a grave) were unable to identify the places with certainty because there were no landmarks and the work was usually done at night in complete darkness.

For that reason, it was astounding that one digger identified a barren field as the final resting place fifteen years after the burial. He was a mere grave-digger. Had he been the killer, he would have made sure to forget the immense, unremarkable field. He thought he remembered the exact place where Gega Kobakhidze was buried years back. Unlike a poet shedding tears over a grave, he did not weep that November night, trying to remember the spot in the moonlight. He had kept the secret for a long time, only to share it fifteen years later with Gega's mother. God knows how many people had whispered to Natela Machavariani that they knew the precise location of her son's grave, but on this occaision her maternal instinct told her that this man was not lying.

The man couldn't be lying. His face was like stone, with all he had seen and experienced in his life hidden behind it. Natela immediately thought he looked dead himself. It was all he knew. For years, 'well-wishers' who claimed they could show her the grave of her son approached Natela. And she followed each and every one on a wild goose chase. Some were sent by the KGB, others demanded a reward and a few just abandoned her at distant railway stations on the way to the barren plains of Siberia.

It's hard to believe in death until you face it. It's even harder to believe in death when it's your child, especially when the authorities have hidden all details about it without an explanation. But there are no bans on dreaming and hoping for the better. Hope belongs to you and only you, helping you through your life, driving you ahead, impelling you to go on with your life.

For many years various people nurtured this hope in Gega's mother, claiming that he was seen in this or that prison or special Siberian camp. Similar claims were made about the other missing members of the group. Parents went to look for their sons. They went not because they believed it was possible to find a trace of their executed sons in this immense, unlawful, terrifying country, but because they feared their hope would die.

And this gravedigger appeared when the hope was about to die.

Other parents, too, decided they preferred to face the truth, however painful it might have been. They decided it was time to know where their sons found their final resting place. So when the gravedigger approached her, Natela immediately guessed he knew much more than others before him. She knew immediately and unerringly he would be the one to bury their hope.

It was a small group, and they went in secret. It was cold and wet, but the women were not afraid to dig alongside the men. The rain stopped from time to time, but the soggy soil was so heavy to dig that the men's raspy breathing carried across the immense, barren, nameless field. Natela was sure the man had remembered the precise place where her son was buried, though the field had long been a mass graveyard for the executed political and criminal convicts of the Soviet regime. They were buried at night, in utter secrecy, without coffins or indications of their names.

Even the gravedigger was surprised to hear his cold spade hit the coffin. Only then did he remember how exceptional it was that an executed prisoner was buried in a coffin. He repeated with more confidence the phrase which brought the parents to the site. He knew Gega Kobakhidze lay there. The coffin was metal as opposed to the traditional wooden ones. Misha, Gega's father, nearly fainted at the clanking sound. The women wanted to give him some water, but they didn't have any and the nearest village was miles away. Strangely enough, no one could say with any certainty which way they had come to the field. On their secret trip, each was trying to memorize the road they followed, but the metallic sound erased everything else from their minds.

They stood on a grassy field as large as a city, while under their feet lay a massive graveyard. It hid the darkest history of 20th century Georgia. The field had accommodated those unwanted by the Soviet authorities, those brought from obscure underground dungeons to their final resting place.

The gravedigger miraculously produced some water for Misha Kobakhidze. Now only minutes distanced them from opening the metal coffin. Gega's parents were spared the last minute, though God only knows how many times they had lived through this very minute in their imagination. The coffin was opened. Natia Megrelishvili immediately recognized the body. It wasn't Gega Kobakhidze.

Before they found the burial site, on that rainy day in 1999, there was next to no hope of finding the grave in this open field. In reply to Natela Machavariani's silent question, the strange-faced man said loudly:

"This is the place, I remember for sure."

"It's been fifteen years now," someone remarked.

"Gega's grave is here, I remember for sure."

The men continued to dig in silence. The sound of their quickened breathing seemed deafening to the parents standing around the hole. One of their spades hit a coffin and everyone froze at the sound, but only for a second. Then they dug the coffin out and lifted it onto the surface.

When the men opened the coffin lid, Gega's mother turned away, waiting for their reaction. The men, deeply stunned, looked at the corpse, which was difficult to identify due to the passing of time. But it was Natia Megrelishvili who said with conviction.

"This isn't Gega. This is Soso. It's his jeans, there's the sun drawn on them."

The others looked at the open coffin again and only now discovered the deceased was wearing the jeans, unaffected after all those years. They still looked new, and there was a shining sun drawn above the right knee.

Eka Chikhladze couldn't have imagined she'd ever see Soso Tsereteli again. He was still in the same pair of jeans she last seen him wearing fifteen years ago, several days before the hijack...

# TINA

Fifteen years earlier, on November 18th 1983, a young woman with a hand grenade stood in the open door of an unsuccessfully hijacked airplane. Her face was streaked with raindrops in expectation of the end.

She stood with a grenade in her hand to bring an end to everything, to make the authorities do whatever they had planned. The end was anxiously awaited after the unbearably lengthy siege of the plane. By then, everyone watching the events from the outside, and those sitting on the inside, could only dream for the end to come quickly. Some passengers and crew members were dead in the bullet-ridden plane, their corpses left lying in the aisle. Others were wounded—their moans interrupting the silence in the plane. One of them begged Tina to not explode the grenade. For a long time, Tina gave no answer. But eventually, as if to herself, she said, with a touch of regret:

"Calm down lady, it isn't even real."

But the lady still looked bewildered with horror, just like the other passengers. Among their faces Tina searched for the one that was the dearest to her. Finally, but only briefly, she found it and looked into Gega's eyes.

Their eyes met for only a second. At that exact moment, special forces stormed in from on the top of the plane and filled the cabin with white smoke.

Ever since her childhood, Tina was stunningly beautiful. Boys made eyes at her and chased her wherever she went; school, art class, English lessons, anywhere.

But when she grew up, it simply began to irritate her. It seemed that boys were mostly interested in her beauty, but Tina always believed she was more interesting. For that reason, it is likely that Tina had never been in love before she met Gega.

Tina was a student of the Fine Arts Academy when Gega saw her painting somewhere, by chance, and made sure to get her number. As an experienced actor, Gega had such a voice that Tina would have believed anything he told her when he reached her on the phone to inquire about her work. He said he really liked her painting, and wanted to meet her. But, he also wanted to be sure to tell Tina, right away, that he was physically handicapped. For a long time afterwards, Gega couldn't explain why he joked about being handicapped, but at the time, Tina's kind reply simply stupefied him.

"It doesn't matter whether you are handicapped or not, personality is the main thing for me."

When he first heard Tina's response, with an angelic voice that was so unlike the rather wild students of Tbilisi's Fine Arts Academy, he hung up immediately. He really hadn't expected such an answer, and didn't think a modern girl living in Tbilisi could be like that. He immediately regretted his crass joke but tried to justify it by the fact that he wanted to hide his true identity. Gega was a young actor, good-looking and extremely talented. Only twenty-two, he had already played successful parts in several films. At the time, he was well known in Georgia and extremely popular in Tbilisi, especially among teenage girls. Gega didn't want to rely on his popularity. It was why he made up the story about being handicapped and stricken to a wheelchair. After he thought it over for a bit longer, he dialed Tina's number again, though he didn't giving up on his phony story.

"Hello?" said Tina in that adorable voice he had already missed. Upon hearing her again, Gega became lost and awkward for a second time. Although Gega was considered a talented young actor, this role was difficult to pull off. He quickly grew embarrassed at his lack of professionalism. He coughed to clear his throat.

"It's me again," he finally managed to say, clearing his throat again.

"Where did you go?" Tina asked with genuine surprise.

"Nowhere. The connection simply cut off."

"What were you saying?"

"When?"

"Before the connection died."

"I was saying that I was handicapped and that I can't move without a wheelchair."

"That's ok, if you don't mind, I can come to your place and bring my paintings."

"Oh, no, I don't want to bother you and also…"

"Also what?"

"Also I am always at home as it is, and I'd prefer to meet somewhere."

"I see. I didn't want to trouble you, but now I am."

"Let's meet wherever you want."

"I'll come to wherever you prefer."

"I'd prefer the Arts Academy after lectures have finished."

"How will you recognize me?"

"Well, you'll easily recognize me. I doubt someone else looking like me is going to have a date in front of the Academy."

"I've already said I understand your situation..."

"But I still think it isn't particularly pleasant that some guy in a wheelchair is waiting for a beautiful girl like you after lectures..."

"A beautiful girl like me? How do you know what I look like?"

"I don't, but whatever you look like, your friends will still be surprised to see your handicapped admirer in front of the Academy."

"My life is my business."

"Tomorrow?"

"Tomorrow what?"

"Can I come tomorrow?"

"Our lectures finish at three tomorrow."

"I'll come by at three. I'll be standing at the monument...I mean sitting."

"I'll come as soon as lectures are over."

"Until tomorrow then."

"I've probably tired you out already."

"Oh, no, how can you say that..."

Gega really wasn't tired but he didn't want to continue the conversation, or rather couldn't continue it, so he said goodbye and hung up. Then he smiled with a strange sense of pleasure. Apparently completely different girls did live in this city, though maybe there are very few of them, maybe only Tina, but still...

Gega also realized that Tina couldn't be lied to anymore, as it really was a bad joke. Tina was the last person he wanted to hurt. He spent the night thinking it over while listening to his favourite records. He decided he would explain everything to Tina when they met at the Academy the next day and would apologize. Though he had already made up his mind, he still couldn't sleep. He kept thinking about Tina's angelic voice?—the girl who wasn't like the others.

At noon the following day, he came by his friend Dato's place. Dato Mikaberidze had a genuine Wrangler denim jacket that Gega prized very much, though he never mentioned this to him. Dato was very generous and would have immediately taken the jacket off and gifted it to Gega. Dato's generosity was not because his father worked at the Ministry (foreigner tourism). He was simply very generous, period.

But that day, Gega decided to ask to borrow that Wrangler jacket for a day, or more precisely, for half a day—he would meet with Tina, apologize and return the denim jacket to Dato in the evening.

He called loudly from the street and Vazha, Dato's younger brother, looked out of the window. Vazha's nickname was 'Simpleton,' but he was a kind person, just like his brother. Gega raised his arm to greet him.

"How are you?"

"Alright."

"Shouldn't you be at school?"

"It burned down."

"When?"

"This morning, it's still burning."

"Wow! Where's your brother?"

"Dunno. He wasn't home when I woke up."

"I guess you were probably woken up by the fire engines…"

They both laughed loudly.

Gega waived goodbye to Simpleton and turned around to leave, but Vazha kept talking.

"Did you want anything?"

"No, nothing, I'll come by later."

"Come on, tell me."

"Nothing special. I just wanted to borrow Dato's Wrangler jacket for a day."

"Hold on."

Simpleton disappeared from the window and seconds later was standing in front of Gega on the street with the jacket in his hand.

"Take it. You're really lucky. Dato wears it all the time but left it behind today."

"No, I'll get it from him later."

"Take it, it's really mine, Dad bought it for me but it was too big for me. Dato only has it for the time being. It's going to be mine anyway. It's a real Wrangler. It's not going to wear out or anything..."

Gega smiled and stretched out his hand to Simpleton. "I will bring it back today."

"Whenever you want. It's still too large for me anyways. If you want, you can have it until I grow up."

Gega laughed loudly.

"And what about Dato?"

"Dato's going to be a monk, he won't need jeans anymore."

Vazha laughed loudly along with Gega, who suddenly remembered that Dato really had a friend at a monastery and often went to see him. Once or twice he had promised to take Gega but so far these were only promises. This was not the time to think about it. He thanked Vazha and gave him a Tbilisi-style hug.

Tbilisi had been the capital for fifteen hundred years, and like in any capital, for all the good things that happened there, there was also a darker side. As Gega left for his date and started to climb up the street that went to the Fine Arts Academy, three men with knives met him and demanded that he take off the jacket.

In those days, old-timers still used to stroll in that part of the city, and so it was a bit strange for a thief to say to Gega:

"Hey, man, come over for a sec, I've got some business with you," as he motioned Gega into the entrance of the residential building. Even stranger for Gega, just as he discovered two more 'happy' guys in the entrance, was that he was not scared at all. Quite the opposite, he found himself smiling, and calmly told them:

"Don't waste your time guys, you can't take it off me anyway!"

Gega was an actor, and in that entrance he spoke very calmly like a person with deep confidence in himself. Such composure surprised Gega. He'd never tried to be a hero and knew perfectly well that in Tbilisi, at that time, it was common for jeans to be taken off people. Like others, he had thought about how he would react in such a situation. Yet he had always thought that he would never let himself be killed if it ever happened, because he wasn't a supporter of senseless heroism, especially when there wasn't a need for it. In another place, in another time, he probably would have silently given over whatever was demanded with a smile, but on that day he acted differently. He reacted differently not only because the denim jacket wasn't his, but because he was on his way to a first date with a girl with a beautiful voice who he hadn't even met yet.

Two of the three thugs had knives, and before abandoning their robbery and running, they managed to stab Gega. In Tbilisi in those days, most knives were aimed at the legs or buttocks, even during fights, but Gega was stabbed in the stomach, as well as his legs. In fact, though he hadn't realized it, they had also cut the jacket in their failed attempt to snatch it away.

When Gega came out into the street, he managed to take a few more steps, but having lost a lot of blood, he soon lost consciousness. He fainted right there, on the pavement.

When he opened his eyes, he was lying in a hospital ward. His mother was crying at the head of the bed, silently and carefully stroking Gega's hand.

"Where is Tina?" Gega asked, looking at his mother. "Who is Tina?" his mother asked, drying her eyes in surprise.

"I don't know, I haven't met her yet," said Gega, smiling at his mother.

Gega was right; he really hadn't met Tina yet. She waited a long time in front of the Fine Arts Academy looking for a man in a wheelchair. But at that same moment Gega was being operated on at the hospital. He would wait days before he called her.

"I'm sorry I couldn't make it, and didn't call you. I'm still in the hospital."

"How nice."

"What's nice?"

"Sorry, I didn't mean it. I wanted to say something else. It's nice you had a valid excuse for not showing up that day."

"I'll meet you as soon as they let me out of here."

"You know, if you don't mind, I'll come see you at the hospital and bring you some fruit, or tell me what you like and what will make you happy."

"No, please don't come here, they'll discharge me soon and I'll see you then. Goodbye."

"I hope you get well soon."

Gega spent several more days in the hospital, and was visited by his friends and acquaintances that treated him like a hero. By then the whole city knew that the thieves had failed to take the jacket off Gega, he stubbornly joked:

"I was trying to give it to them, but they wouldn't let me."

With this repeated remark, he wanted to make clear that he wasn't a hero. A year later, sitting on death row in Tbilisi's Ortachala prison, Gega often remembered his hospital days when they wanted to make a hero out of him and he wanted to just be an ordinary person.

They didn't keep him in the hospital for long, though he still found it difficult to walk. According to the doctors, his full recovery was only a matter of time. After the operation, Gega's friends, the Iverieli brothers, who studied at the medical college, managed to get a wheelchair for him. In the evenings, when he was finally left alone, tired of all the praise, he would roll in his wheelchair to a black telephone hung on a pink wall at the end of the corridor and call Tina.

He met up with her the day after he was discharged. He went to the Academy in his wheelchair; this time he really couldn't move around without it. However, Tina was irked by his initial fib about the wheelchair and didn't talk to him for a week, though he called her every day. Gega attempted to come up with some kind of explanation, but Tina wouldn't speak to him, though she didn't hang up either. Staying silent, she just listened to Gega talk.

Gega struggled to explain a joke he could hardly explain to himself. Indeed, it was a twist of fate or karma that turned Gega's poorly executed joke into reality when he was forced to go on his first date with Tina in a wheel-chair.

Eventually, Gega returned the wheelchair to the Iverieli brothers, who returned it to the hospital.

Dato flatly refused to take back the Wrangler jacket (the blood was carefully scrubbed out and the tear carefully mended by Gega's mother) and promised to give Gega a new pair jeans.

Yet Gega didn't want anything but Tina, and thought of nothing else. Only Tina—the most beautiful girl in the world...

# SOSO'S FATHER

Soso's Father was a famous professor, one of the best scientists of his era. Unlike the previous generation, in the 1960s and '70s they didn't execute professors and scientists anymore. In return for their lives, the Soviet authorities forced them to cooperate. Most of them did, since the alternative meant never being able to travel abroad to attend important scientific conferences. Such cooperation, at first glance, was nothing special. Sometimes, nothing was requested in return for permission to take foreign trips, but this was superficial. In reality, freedom of speech and the right to self-expression were prohibited. Scientists and professors couldn't openly express political views and had to always support the government. That's what really happened. Of course, there were exceptions—those who didn't want the privileges, apartments and cars given out by the government. Yet there were very few of these people. Mostly, they sat in the kitchens of their council flats. Only there, in the

safety of their tiny homes, would they express negative opinions about the Soviet regime. Some academics chose not to
speak in the comfort of their kitchens. They were labeled
dissidents and thrown in jail.

Soso's father was not one of these. He was one of the
most prominent scientists in Soviet Georgia—an academician who was treated with special respect by Eduard Shevardnadze, the First Secretary of the Central Committee
of the Communist Party. Soso hated his father's close and
warm relations with the authorities.

For the liberal and anti-Soviet Tbilisi youth like Soso, Shevardnadze was a completely unacceptable figure, regarded
as just another power-crazy communist. Although promo-
tion and career-building in the Soviet Union required little
intelligence or education, it involved something else, and
Shevardnadze had it. Having started his career in a beautiful village in Guria, he climbed to the top of the Soviet
hierarchy. In the beginning of the 1970s, thanks to his zeal,
Shevardnadze reached the top of the Georgian government
and easily, managed to charm the country's intelligentsia.
This was helped by the fact that for years the intellectual
abilities of the so-called Soviet intelligentsia had been dete-
riorating (alongside their morals). When Shevardnadze came
to power, and immediately started arresting underground
entrepreneurs in the black market, the Georgian intelligentsia was delighted because they believed that the arrests of
people like Otar Lazishvili were an attempt to fight corruption. They failed to realize that the black market, though
illegal, was still key to the foundation of the economy.

Aside from the fact that Soviet-era underground business-
men were extremely daring individuals, they were also
gifted people that helped form the middle class. While Shevardnadze won over the intelligentsia with his fight against

supposed corruption and the black market, younger Georgians understood that he was an extremely dangerous man. People like Soso hated Shevardnadze, and couldn't understand why scientist like his father needed to cooperate with such people.

Soso was a student at the Fine Arts Academy and dreamed of financially independence after graduation so he could leave his parents. Soso practically never talked to his father anymore and hardly talked to his mother. She always tried to preserve a peaceful family atmosphere, but what was virtually impossible.

Soso pitied his father. He wouldn't talk to him anymore, only answering his questions. Before going to the United States to a seminar, his father asked him what to bring him from abroad. Soso simply smiled in reply:

"Nothing," he said very calmly.

But his father, whom he had madly loved from his early childhood, now looked miserable, so Soso added:

"Thank you."

His father didn't say anything else. He already knew what to bring him. He had students, and was keenly aware that the dream of any Georgian youth was a pair of genuine American jeans. For his son's sake, Soso's father decided to be brave on his next foreign trip for the first time. As soon as the KGB-employed minder let his attention wander, he would buy real jeans for Soso, even though it scared him stiff.

He was mostly afraid of the uncertainty. He didn't really know what the punishment was for bringing American jeans into the country. He could be severely punished, or there could be an official reprimand entered into his private record. He could be fired from his position as the Institute Director and expelled from the Party. In that case, there would be TV coverage. Anonymous letters might appear in the press, saying a Soviet academician had been unable to resist the Western temptation and fell for the capitalist lure of Americans jeans. Any letter, or news anchor, would conclude with remarks that: "This is how a Georgian scientist appreciates the efforts of the government. This is how he betrays our country for a pair of cheap trousers."

When Soso's father bought the jeans, he could hear this voice ringing in his head. Yet, he was happy that he had finally used some free choice for the first time in his life. Then again, the jeans weren't as cheap as he thought they would be. They were quite expensive, especially considering the limited funds officially allowed for scientists on trips abroad. Any fee allotted from a public lecture was alwys kept by the authorities. But still, the purchase itself wasn't the main scare. It was crossing the border control at the airport on the way back. Again, he could hear the voices in his head. For a split second he even thought of taking the jeans out of his luggage and turning himself in, but he managed to build up his courage and dried his sweaty palms. In reply to the Russian border guard's question about bringing anything illegal goods into the country, Soso's father smiled at the guard:

"It's hot," he said, as he dried his forehead with a handkerchief.

The border guard failed to notice the sweat and repeated his question.

"Nothing," replied Soso's father, without much conviction. "Of course not, nothing that's forbidden," he added with more conviction.

The border guard looked at him with such penetrating eyes that he was reminded of his students during exams.

"Shall we have a look?" The border guard asked him as he looked down at the scientist's suitcase.

Soso's father didn't trust his voice, so he simply nodded. The only thing he could think of was the cardiac pills he had in his pocket, but he would need to put the medicine under his tongue without the border guard noticing. It wasn't that easy—the pain began to spread from his heart through his whole body and wouldn't stop.

When Soso's father opened his eyes, everything was already over—a woman in a white coat was feeling his pulse, shaking her head ruefully.

"You've traveled a long way, so no wonder you're exhausted. Also, I hope you don't mind me saying so, but you're not a young man anymore and you shouldn't be taking long trips."

He didn't know what had really happened at the airport, whether his luggage was checked or not, but when he returned home he found the jeans were still in his bag. What worried Soso's father the most was that they might have spotted them and said nothing.

He said nothing to his wife or son about the incident. Instead, silently and proudly, he handed the genuine American jeans to his son. Soso simply smiled and thanked his father, but inside he kept thinking about how much worry it must have caused his father to cross the border with them.

Soso mother asked her son to try on the jeans for her to see if they fit but Soso only smiled, kissed his mother and locked himself in his room. He wasn't a little boy anymore.

He spent the whole night painting and listening to Led Zeppelin. Once in a while he would glance over at his new jeans hanging on a chair below the Mick Jagger poster on the wall. When he became tired, he smoked a cigarette, but he still didn't try the jeans on. It was dawn by the time he fell asleep.

He didn't even have breakfast in the morning. He tucked the jeans under his arm and went to see his friend Irakli Kostava.

Irakli was the son of the well-known Georgian dissident, Merab Kostava. Merab, a man of amazing integrity and absolute resolve, was serving the fourth year of his sentence in some remote Siberian camp for his anti-Soviet activities. Soso knew that Irakli's father would never be able to bring his son real American jeans and would not be coming back to Georgia for a long time. So it didn't take Soso long to make his decision before he went off to see Irakli.

Irakli had been writing poetry, and had hardly slept. When he saw the jeans, he rubbed his sleepy eyes repeatedly before he finally believed that the jeans were really his. When he eventually realized what he was being given, he smiled, hugged Soso and quietly, but very convincingly, told him:

"I can't take them."

Soso had known this would happen, because of Irakli's pride, and had an answer ready:

"If you don't take them, I'm going to tear them up."

"Are they real?" Irakli asked with a laugh.

"Authentic and American," said Soso, with a trace of resentment in his voice.

"Then you can't tear them up, real jeans don't tear."

"Then I'll burn them!"

"They don't burn either, and they're waterproof," said Irakli, laughing again.

For almost a year Irakli had worn some authentic jeans his friend had given him. When he wore them, people on the streets of Tbilisi followed him with their eyes, while teenagers came up to him to take a closer look.

Soso was surprised, so Iralki explained:

"I'm just extremely tired and very sick of it," he said, apologizing to his friend.

Soso thought he was talking about the jeans, but when he heard about his suicide the next day, he understood what he had meant. When he heard the news, he initially thought Irakli had beaten them all, but then he grew angry with himself as he thought about the previous day and how he hadn't noticed that anything was wrong. Then he cried like a child.

After Irakli Kostava's funeral, Soso put on Irakli's jeans and drew a shining sun above the left knee. He wore them up to his own death.

He was buried in those jeans, in secret. They would help Natia Megrelishvili identify his corpse fifteen years later...

# GEGA

Gega's father was also a well-known and successful Georgian film director who had made wonderful films when he was still very young. He was one of the first Georgians (as far back as the 1960s) to win prestigious international film festivals prizes. But even back then, he was a real artist and his passion was the creative process. He didn't relish the prizes and awards. For this reason, unlike many Georgian directors of the older generation, Gega's father refused to conform with many Soviet intellectuals supporting the regime. He lived only through the cinema. But it wasn't in the interests of the Soviet authorities to allow such a standard. They hated having no control over a film director and consequently solved the issue by banning Gega's father from making films. Needless to say, there was no official decree from the Central Committee that forbade this, but it was explained unofficially that he wouldn't be given the opportunity to make films any longer. The Soviet authorities relied on the conformity of the

Georgian intelligentsia and utilized it. But Gega's father was a very determined man. He learned the craft of carpentry and began making wooden floors. Much of Georgian society at the time regarded such a trade to be something unseemly and shameful. They looked on with indignation at a man who refused to conform or curry favour with the government and the Party. Gega's father, on the other hand, was convinced that what was truly shameful was blindly conforming like so many in the Georgian intelligentsia. There was much gossip and chatter; nobody knew for certain whether Gega's father was really working as a carpenter or if it was some kind of myth concocted by those looking for a true voice in the fight against the Soviet government.

It was his son Gega who was a true talent. Thanks to his gift for acting, and many successful roles, he was invited by Tengiz Abuladze to play the lead role in his new film. Then, a girl appeared in his life that was bigger than any film.

This was Tina. Though their first meeting was strange and their relationship began with a row, Gega was madly in love from the beginning. After they made up from their first fight, they went on their first real date. Tina asked that it take away from the rest of the city, just the two of them, and so they met at dawn, on Rustaveli Avenue. The street was completely deserted. Unlike Gega, who was a little miffed and very sleepy (he had never got up this early) at the early morning rendezvous, Tina seemed pleased. She sat next to Gega on a long bench and looked onat the solitary street-sweeper lazily moving down the street. He swept silently, with only the sound of the autumn leaves breaking the silence. Gega felt the morning stillness, and looked at Tina. With her head bent low, as if afraid to wake the whole city, she whispered:

"It's just the two of us in this city right now—you and me. Nobody else."

"Three of us," Gega said with a smile as he looked at the street-sweeper.

Tina paid no attention to the joke and whispered again: "In this city, in the whole world, there's only the two of us..."

It made Gega remember that the French film *Two In Town* was in every cinema in Tbilisi, but he didn't dare make another joke. He understood that he could easily lose this girl with another joke, maybe forever.

So he pondered for a while and then asked, this time not in a whisper so that Tina could hear:

"Only the two of us?"

"Only two of us: you and me. Do you want it?"

"Yes."

"Can you?"

"Yes."

"Can you see me tomorrow morning, but earlier than today?"

"Earlier? Earlier than this ... It's still dark."

"Before dawn, let's meet and go up to Mtatsminda."

"Shall we walk?"

"Yes... and we'll watch the sunrise. Do you want to?"

"Yes," said Gega hesitatingly. Although he knew, for certain, that he didn't really fancy walking up the steep slope to watch the sunrise.

The first car of the day passed down the street and its driver stared with surprise at the couple sitting on a bench so early in the morning.

"Let's go," said Tina as she stood up.

That afternoon, Dato came by Gega's place and woke him up. Gega's mother, Natela, was glad to see Dato, since her son had been sleeping the whole day and was supposed to go to the theatre in the evening.

"He left at dawn, then came back, had some tea and has been sleeping ever since," Gega's mother told Dato.

By then, she already knew that her son was in love of course, and noisily opened the door to his room for Dato. Dato loudly clapped his hands, and slyly asked his drowsy friend as soon as they were alone:

"Are you in love?"

"Who told you?" Gega asked as he rubbed his eyes and sat up.

"*Voice Of America* has already broadcast it," Dato merrily said as he pointed to the American flag hanging on the wall.

"I've got to get up early tomorrow as well."

"Your mom told me you got up at dawn today."

"I have to get up earlier than that tomorrow. Before sunrise. We're climbing up to Mtatsminda."

"To take a look at Stalin's mum's grave?"

"To watch the sunrise."

"I've never even noticed which direction the sun rises in Tbilisi."

"Have you ever even looked at the sky in Tbilisi?"

"I might have."

"Do you remember the last time you looked up at the sky?"

"No…"

"That's the main drawback of cities. You can't see the sky."

A little baffled, Dato went to the window, looked up at the sky and asked Gega with a smile:

"Did she tell you that?"

"I figured it out myself," Gega smiled as he joined him at the window.

"You really can't see the sky from here."

"Because the building in front is taller than this one."

"What do people who live in New York do?"

"I wish I lived in New York, I'd never even look up at the sky."

"Before you get to New York, maybe you want to come along to the monastery. Come at least once. Soso's coming with us on Saturday. At least you'll be able to see the sky if you miss it so much. It is a great place."

"I told you where I'm going tomorrow. I'll go with you next week."

For a while they were both silent, then Dato changed the subject:

"Where's the police station?"

"The police station is on the other side, where the yard is. If it was on this side, I wouldn't be able to sleep at night."

"Why?"

"At night, they beat people in there and such horrible sounds escape that people who lived in the flats facing the yard sold them and moved out."

"What do you mean they beat people?"

"Torture them."

"Who?"

"Criminals. Well... you know, they never arrest innocent people here and..."

Dato became so serious and distressed that Gega didn't finish his sentence and instead smiled at his friend:

"I'm joking, don't worry."

"I know."

"But I still don't recommend you ever find yourself in a police station," Gega said.

"We're off," he called to his mother.

She came out of the other room and said goodbye to Dato before straightening the crumpled collar of Gega's jacket. Gega kissed his mother, as he always did when leaving home. After she locked the door, Natela looked out from the window at her son as he appeared at the building's entrance. As always, Gega knew his mother was watching him, so he jokingly raised his left leg as a sign of goodbye, without looking back.

It was still dark when Gega found made it to beneath the third floor window of Tina's room, where a light was on and her silhouette appeared for a second in the frame. When the light went out, Gega took out a cigarette and lit it. The sound of hurrying feet could be heard on the stairs and as she appeared from the entrance, Tina smiled at Gega and thanked him.

"Thanks for what?" he asked with sincere surprise.

"For waking up. Getting up this early isn't easy at all," Tina said as she walked down the pavement smiling.

"Depends on the case, or rather, for whose sake," said Gega, although he knew perfectly well that getting up so early was really very difficult for him and he found it extremely hard.

Tina said nothing in reply and smiled at Gega as if careful not to disturb the night's silence. When they went up the old cobbled streets of Tbilisi, the silence was broken only by the sound of their steps. The ascent was long, and Gega was sure he would soon tire, but he didn't. The chill of the dawn even felt good to him, especially when he looked down at the still sleeping city.

The sun, meanwhile, slowly rose upwards in the Tbilisi sky, and Gega felt like thanking Tina for bringing him up this hill. Her face radiated such happiness at the tranquility around, and Gega now understood that silence was more precious than words. He only broke it on the way back, when they were coming down from Mtatsminda:

"Are we going to watch the sunset from here as well?"

"You can't see the sunset from here."

"Then what are we going to do?"

"Go to the sea."

"Now? To the sea?"

"The sea is at its best now, the autumn sea."

"Will anyone be there?"

"Only you, me and the sea. What do you say?"

"Yes," said Gega as he hesitantly touched Tina's fingers with his right hand.

It was already morning, and people began to appear in the street. Several girls, heading to school in their uniforms, stared back to look at the beautiful couple. What they didn't know was, that when Tina and Gega's fingers touched for the first time that morning, they felt like the most beautiful people in the world.

# THE MONK

"I'm sorry, but I can't go any farther. The car's not gonna make it," the driver told his passengers as he switched off the engine. They all got out, dragging their backpacks.

"Is it far from here?" Soso asked as he looked up at the mountain top.

"We'll be there in an hour, even sooner if we walk quickly," Dato said.

"Shall we let the driver go then? There's fresh snow and the car's really going to be in trouble for nothing," Paata said.

"If I had chains on my wheels, I'd take you. But there's no way it's going up without them, I know that for sure. It's a Soviet car..."

The driver was clearly pleased at having the lads agree so easily. He eagerly took the money from Dato, who hurriedly started up the snowy slope. The others slowly followed

27

him. Soso even paused several times to take in the scenic white valley.

"There's a scene for one of your paintings," Kakhaberber said to Soso with a smile, still surprised at the early snow.

"It really is very early to have snowed here," Soso agreed. They didn't talk further, knowing it would only tire them as they climbed.

Soon, the monastery appeared. It was so beautiful against the background of white mountains that they all stopped. Soso smiled and more to himself than to others, uttered his favourite phrase:

"He's still the greatest painter..."

"Who?" asked Paata.

Soso didn't answer, he only pointed at the monastery's entrance where a robed monk was standing with a little girl, looking at the guests. Then, the monk and girl came down the hill to meet the hikers on the road. Greeting his guests, the monk hugged Dato and the brothers, and then firmly shook Soso's hand.

"This is Soso, our friend the painter, the one I told you about, who wanted to come," Dato told the monk. Everyone took off their backpacks.

"May God turn all your roads into the road of virtue," the monk said, mostly to Soso as he tried to carry his backpack.

"We're almost there," Soso said, not letting the monk take his bag. He carried his backpack up to the monastery, where its white yard was a really wonderful sight. There were only a few small rooms left at the monastery, and a larger refectory, where the boys put their food so they could prepare a meal.

Before they ate, the monk said the Lord's Prayer and made a cross. The group followed his example, including little Eka, who said the Lord's Prayer together with her father as she looked up at him with a pleased expression.

During the meal, she behaved like a true hostess, showing such hospitality to her father's guests that they couldn't help smiling. Her father was quite proud of his little hostess and praised her several times. In appreciation, the little lady affectionately kissed her father. Then, Dato broke the silence and said what must have been on everyone's mind:

"So strange it's snowed here so early. We're still having a warm autumn in Tbilisi."

"This is what our country is like," said the monk, Father Tevdore. "It's a small place, but wonderful. There's already snow here while down at the seaside they are probably still sunbathing. The Lord has given everything to this small country, while the people have lost their sense of gratitude and have forgotten him."

"Why?" Soso interrupted. "People in this country still remember God, even though they are forbidden to even go to Church. This country has a bad government, it's not the people's fault at all..."

"The government also consists of people," the monk responded, "and the government is part of the people who you are now praising."

"I'm not praising anyone. I'm simply defending those who have no right to choose and who, consequently, aren't responsible for the people in the government. The right to make a decision has been taken away from people. That's why they shouldn't be held responsible for what's happening in our country," Soso said angrily as he glanced at his friends. They looked calm, well aware that Soso always liked to argue, though not to fight. He never insulted his challenger and kept his arguments well-grounded.

"Do you think that if this country had a government elected by the people and not appointed by the Kremlin, as it is now, it would be less atheistic and not as bad?" Father Tevdore calmly asked as he filled his empty wine glass for him. The monk's stillness was contagious, calming Soso immediately and responded with a smile.

"Good or bad, if the people elect their government, then they're responsible, and not some omnipotent leader. It may turn out quite the opposite and the elected government could begin persecuting non-believers, as happens now, but the atheists…"

"I can't even imagine such a Georgia," Dato uttered.

"It's not difficult to imagine it at all. Those attending parades now could be going to churches en masse and crossing themselves every time they see a church…"

"And what's bad about that?" Paata asked Soso, with apparent surprise.

"When done as a show, for the sake of a lie to each other, going to a parade or going to church is equally bad."

"I think it's still better to go to church," said Paata's brother as he looked over at Father Tevdore.

The monk answered all of them at once, though his explanation was mainly for Soso's benefit:

"If someone goes to church, even if only for others to see, it is still better because they will have more time to think about God, and the truth. To think about love, which we all lack."

"Collective thinking always ends in hatred, not love," Soso interrupted again, but Father Tevdore continued unruffled.

"It is true that collective thinking always results in regimes, not freedom, but you can begin your road to freedom by going to church…"

"And then continue it alone like yourself?" Soso asked.

"I prefer to look for my freedom here, far from the city, where there is less noise and a more time to think about God."

"And how long do you intend to stay here?" Dato asked Father Tevdore, though his friends also wanted to know.

"I'll be thirty-three next year, and I wish to be here then, unless they forbid me."

"Who?"

"They have been here already, came up three days ago. But so far they haven't forbidden anything, just looked at the books and left."

"When are they going to bar you?"

"When they consider that my being here is dangerous for them."

"Why?"

"Because fearful people tend to exaggerate, and those without faith are extremely cowardly."

The monk smiled and pointed at little Eka peacefully asleep at the table next to her father.

"She's tired," Paata said, taking little Eka in his arms.

"I think I also have tired you all," Father Tevdore said as he stood up.

The others also got to their feet and said their thanks.

"Please, take Eka with you tomorrow, her school's starting. I'll come at the end of the week and see you in Tbilisi," Father Tevdore said to Dato as they walked into the monastery yard.

"I think we brought you enough food to last a week," Dato said and looked up at the star-studded sky.

"I'll make it last, no problem. The main thing is that you brought honey."

"You like honey?" Soso asked the monk.

"There's a deer that comes here and I feed it honey."

"How?" Dato asked, genuinely surprised.

"With my hand."

"I thought deer liked salt and sour things, not sweet," Soso said.

"I used to think so too. It might be true and only this deer likes honey. I put it in my cupped palm and it licks it."

"What a bright night," Paata said, coming out into the yard and looking up at the sky.

"Kant must have been inspired by such a starry sky."

"I'd like to ask you something," Soso turned to the monk abruptly.

"Sure," Father Tevdore said, "just don't be so formal with me."

"Ok," Soso said. "Where will you go if they forbid you to stay here?"

"I'll go to another monastery."

"What if they don't allow you into another monastery?"

"I'll go to another country and look for my share of peace and quiet there," said Father Tevdore with a smile.

"And what if they don't allow you go to another country?" asked Soso, returning the smile.

"I'll find a way to stealthily creep away," the monk said, laughing. "Now, with your permission, I am going to creep away to get some sleep. I have to get up early in the morning. Also, Eka is alone and if she happens to wake up, she may get scared."

"Eka will surely never be scared of anything," Dato said, laughing and together with the others said goodbye to Father Tevdore.

When the lads were left alone in the monastery yard, they remained silent for a long time, smoking. Then Kakhaberber broke the quiet and asked Soso:

"What do you say?"

"What should I say?"

"Will he agree?"

"I don't know, I don't think so. Let's not tell him anything yet," said Soso and quickly changed the subject:

"What was it that Kant said? What was it that surprised him?"

"*The star-studded sky above me and the morals in me,*" one of them said. The group once againt looked up at the large, shining stars and the unusually pale moon.

"You can hitch-hike. If not, the Tbilisi bus will come by at three," Father Tevdore told them the next morning. He hugged each of them separately and gave many kisses to his little Eka. When they started to descend the slope, he once again made the sign of cross at all of them from a distance. From the road, little Eka waved several times back at her father.

That evening, the silence of the snowy monastery was replaced by a terrible noise. Soso was at his friend's place, where there was a party for the host's birthday. There was much drinking, and people were quite drunk. Although the birthday boy was the drunkest, he still demanded that everybody fill their wine-glasses and listen to his toasts, but no one was paying attention except Soso. Girls were dancing and screaming. Soso really wanted another drink, and didn't want to listen to the toasts. Drunk and tired, Soso grew tired of the toasts, asked the toastmaster:

"Come on, let's drink..."

The toastmaster raised his glass, but soon put it back down and sighed.

"Dammit, I can't take anymore." He sat down, put his head in his hands and fell asleep.

Soso smiled, took away the glass he was hugging, then took a deep breath before putting it to his lips. Gega approached him with a smile and put his arm around his shoulder, took the glass away without a word and poured the remaining wine into another empty glass.

"What do you want?" Soso asked, motioning that he wanted a cigarette.

"I need to talk to you, let's smoke on the balcony."

Soso felt too lazy to go out, but he still followed Gega and began to smoke on the balcony. As the noise of dancing and screaming drifted out from inside, Gega closed the door behind them.

"Did you see him?" he asked Soso as he lit a cigarette.

"Who?"

"Father Tevdore."

"I did."

"And?"

"And what?"

"Did you talk?"

"We did."

"What about?"

"Kant."

"Did you go up there to talk about Kant?"

"I'll tell you about it tomorrow, ok?"

"Knowing your hangovers, you'll be dead tomorrow."

"Tomorrow is November 7th, every decent man should be dead like me."

"Why?"

"To skip it."

"Is that why you drank so much?"

"I had forgot. I wasn't even going to drink, but then I saw red banners being hung on the way here."

"Where?"

"Everywhere."

"Let's go home, Tina and I will see you home."

"I want to drink more."

"You don't need anymore, if you drink more you might skip the whole month of November..."

Soso smiled, and Gega understood that his friend had agreed to go home.

The three of them went down the stairs together, humming to themselves, but Soso still lost his step. Tina and Gega took hold of him from both sides and Soso asked with a smile:

"Am I that drunk?"

He put his arms around them both and was happy his friend was in love. They stopped a taxi and Soso hummed all the way to his house. When he was getting out of the car, he hugged the driver and asked him with a serious face:

"Want me to take a message on your behalf to the New York cabdrivers?"

The driver smiled and answered: "My regards..."

"I can manage myself," Soso said to Tina and Gega at the door.

"We're going to the sea for a week," said Gega.

Soso was surprised. "Now? Try not to freeze."

"How can we freeze if we're together?" Gega put his arm around Tina and kissed her.

"You are too beautiful for this government, be careful," said Soso.

"What?"

"You are too beautiful for the authorities, Soso repeated as he climbed the stairway of his place.

Tina and Gega didn't take another taxi. They walked down the street, with both sides adorned with fluttering red Soviet flags. It was already late, and the lovers silently continued down the empty street. Suddenly, Gega stopped and looked up at a red flag with a smile. Tina knew right away what he intended to do. She smiled as Gega quickly climbed up one of the poles to tear down a flag. He took hold of it, tugged it lightly at first, and was about to try the second time when policemen riding a motorcycle suddenly stopped under the pole. Gega and Tina were surprised, and didn't even understand how a patrol had suddenly and noiselessly appeared on an empty street. Whether it was fear or confusion, the couple was dumbfounded.

"Come down, boy!" barked the mustached policeman sitting at the wheel, switching off his engine. The second policeman was heavy to the point of being obese. Tina even wondered how someone so fat could fit into the seat, though it was the wrong time to think about that. The mustached cop beckoned Gega to come down with his finger, while the fat one pulled out a tin of pickles and bit one, noisily munching. Gega climbed down, gave a strained smile to the silent Tina and looked closely at the mustached policeman, who asked him severely:

"What were you doing up there?"

"I was kissing the flag, commander," Gega said.

Suddenly it seemed possible that he could joke with these two.

"Are you laughing at us?" asked the mustached one sternly, looking over at his partner. The fat policeman was crunching on another pickle, but not taking his eyes off Gega. As if trying to place his face, he suddenly cried:

"You, boy, aren't you an actor? I've seen you in the movies, the one when you wanted get married and your brothers won't let you, isn't that you?"

"Yes," Gega nodded to the fat policeman, "it's me, I'm an actor."

"I was like that too when my older brother wouldn't let me get married, saying he should be first. If I had listened to him, I would still be single."

The fat policeman bit another pickle and looked at his partner, "Let him go, he's a good boy."

Before starting their motorcycles, the mustached policeman looked at Tina, then up at Gega:

"Don't mess with that flag son, they don't like such things and they won't spare you."

"Thank you," said Tina. But the policemen didn't hear. They were already off on their motorcycles, with the Soviet engines roaring in the empty streets.

# THE FIRST

The Georgians have always liked saying that there's nothing accidental in this world. With this in mind, it is important to mention the period when Soso rented a small cozy flat on Lvov Street. The place was basically a bedsit, accommodating a group of friends who regularly socialized at night. The living room on Lvov Street was meant to be Soso's temporary studio, but with all the boarders living there, he could paint only half the day. With little time to work, Dato helped with the rent, sometimes paying for the whole month. Besides having money, Dato had a heart of gold.

One evening on Lvov Street, before they began to discuss the possibility of a hijack, the friends reminisced about the events of April 14th 1978. It was a day when the streets of Tbilisi were packed with people protesting the Kremlin's decision to remove the constitutional status of the Georgian language in favour of Russian. The rally famously reached

such a scale that it forced Moscow to reconsider their decision. As they talked about how to escape from the USSR,
no one could later recall who mentioned the word 'hijack'
first. They were unable to recollect this detail even when
they were locked in KGB cells and had time to go over all
the stages of their plan. They failed to answer the recurring
question during long interrogations: "Who was the first to
mention a hijack?" They weren't asked to provide reasons for
why they wanted to flee the USSR. Supposedly, every Soviet
police officer knew that answer all too well.

That evening on Lvov Street, several nonviolent methods
of fleeing the USSR were tossed around before a hijack was
mentioned. Nothing was said about the reasons for escape.
Everyone in the group agreed that it was impossible to stay
in the country where their human rights were neglected,
voices of opposition sat in prison and the media was tightly
controlled. For young artists or innovators, any creative ini-
tiative was subject to harsh KGB censorship. All of these
were reasons to want to escape from the USSR. Yet that evening, as they sat in that rented room heavy with cigarette
smoke, none of the gathered friends mentioned them aloud.

Their memories of that evening were strange. They could
all remember the discussion, and could recount every single detail to the investigators, except for that one detail.

They remembered listening to *Dark Side of the Moon*,
which Gega had brought over. They recalled arguments
about various alternative methods for fleeing. Eventually,
they agreed that any method other than a hijacking was a
waste of time and effort.

The argument seemed watertight; there was no other
way. In Georgia, it was impossible to get travel visas to
Western countries except in the rare cases where you had
influential parents. It was more realistic to go to one of the
East European countries but, they reasoned, what was to

use of moving from one prison to another, even if the latter was slightly better? Back in the '20s, up until 1929, the border between the USSR and Turkey was only partially controlled and hundreds of Georgians took advantage of the security slackness to cross the border. Inhabitants of the mountainous region of Achara were familiar with all the mountain paths and clandestine routes into northern Turkey and would help for the right price. Those who made it then moved on to Europe.

But by 1929, this escape route was blocked forever.

After World War II, the so-called 'Iron Curtain' was truly impossible to lift, even an inch. In the 1950s, some embarked on a seemingly inhuman task of swimming the Black Sea. Amongst several decades of failed attempts, there was evidence of at least one successful attempt. A Russian from Batumi managed to reach the Turkish shore, probably because he was a professional swimmer. However, he was immediately arrested by the Turkish police and put in prison for three years because no one believed a Soviet citizen could swim all the way to Trabzon without the KGB helping him. He was accused of spying, even after he suggested he swim from Trabzon to Istanbul along the seashore to demonstrate his skill and physical abilities.

But that summer evening in 1983, when Soso and Gega's friends got together on Lvov Street, they could only discuss these escape attempts as myths and legends. The idea of escaping by swimming was far-fetched at best.

Then someone mentioned a hijack as another peaceful option of escape. They argued there was no need for violence, or risk of casualties, as they would only use weapons to threaten the pilots. The plan sounded so simple that some smiled, while others thought it was a joke. It was maybe the fantastic and unlikely nature of the plan that helps explain why no one was able to later recall the author of the suggestion. Throughout the nine months of close interrogation and imprisonment, every single detail of their plan came out. But without exception, everyone completely forgot the simple detail that was crucial to the investigation. The prisoners might have erased it from their memory the moment they heard it. As the investigation wrapped up, the authorities gathered every other fact and feature of that evening on Lvov Street except one—who said it first?

# GIORGI

"Take him for a while, will you?" Manana asked her husband in a very tired voice. Giorgi took the baby who had already been crying nonstop for an hour.

Manana closed the bedroom door and sat down on a chair in the kitchen. She was about to light a cigarette, but changed her mind because the baby had begun to cry harder. Manana went back into the room.

"Give him to me," she told Giorgi and took the baby back again.

"What should I do?" Giorgi asked his wife vaguely, as Manana answered exactly as he expected:

"Nothing."

It was more the voice of a tired woman than that of an angry wife. Giorgi went to the kitchen, opened the small window and lit a cigarette. He smoked it quickly and nervously because, like any young father, it was baby's crying which drove him crazy more than anything else.

41

Normally he had a calmer disposition and could put up these things.

He smoked the cigarette till the end and then opened the fridge. It was empty. He closed the door in dismay, stifling the urge to curse. But his frustration quickly subsided when he tiptoed to the bedroom door. The baby had stopped crying. Giorgi carefully lifted the curtain hanging on the door to the bedroom. Mother and child were both asleep.

Giorgi lit another cigarette, more relaxed this time, and opened the little window again. He didn't throw the stub out of the window as he usually did, but extinguished it under the tap. He lifted the lid of the trashcan, very carefully, and threw the stub away. Then he opened the empty fridge and closed it again.

"Surprised it's empty?" asked his wife.

Giorgi turned around quickly. "I thought you were asleep," he said as he sat down on a chair.

"I was, but I have to prepare food for the baby."

"It might be his earache again."

"It might."

"Don't you have that medicine anymore?"

"No, and I can't borrow it from the neighbours anymore either."

"I'll buy some tomorrow."

"With what?"

"I'll buy it."

"Are you going to borrow again?"

"I'll buy it."

"It's hard to find too."

"I'll get it from Chashka."

"It'll be very expensive at Chashka's."

"I'll buy it."

"Let's have some tea. Have you done anything about the job?"

"They'll tell me tomorrow."

"Will they take you?"

"Probably."

"They won't take you anywhere. Why do you hope they will?"

"They don't know about my criminal record."

"Even if they did, you were officially acquitted, you even have that rehabilitation sheet in your personal file."

"No one ever looks at that sheet."

"And you, of course, never tell them to read all the documents to the end."

"Of course."

"Your dignity and self-respect wouldn't allow that."

"I can't beg."

"Why do you hope these people will take you then?"

"I took out from the file what was unnecessary, before giving it to the staff department."

The husband and wife both started laughing, but immediately remembered their child, and put their hands over their mouths.

"I'll fry some potatoes quickly," Manana told Giorgi. "There are still some left and it's not too much trouble."

"I'm not hungry," Giorgi said as he lit another cigarette on the gas fire and opened the little window.

In the morning, Giorgi left home early. He looked at the parcel under his arm, once again, and took the trolley-bus to Lenin Square. From the square, he walked down Leselidze Street and turned towards the synagogue.

Several Jews were standing in front of the synagogue and Giorgi asked them if they had seen Chashka by any chance. They were reluctant to talk to a complete stranger. What business could Giorgi have with Chashka? He hadn't seen him before but knew, like everyone in Tbilisi, that Chashka was selling foreign medicine that was hard to find locally.

Giorgi didn't know what Chashka looked like, but he intuitively felt that Chashka was standing there at the moment, so he stated his reason directly:

"I need medicine for a child."

With his intuition and experience, Chashka knew this man was a real client and not someone from the KGB or other agency. He approached Giorgi.

"Come on," he told him, leading him into the ground-floor flat of a nearby house. Chashka opened a notepad and offered a chair to his visitor. Out of curiosity, Giorgi tried to look around the room, but Chashka cut to the chase:

"What medicine do you want?" he asked as he looked into his notepad again.

"German eardrops, I need it for a child. He hasn't slept for three nights. A neighbour gave us some Bulgarian stuff, but we've used it all."

"That Bulgarian stuff is no good, you need either German or French," Chashka interrupted him, accompanying his words with a gesture meaning, "there's nothing else one can do."

"Have you got it?" Giorgi was so nervous for the answer that he was about to light a cigarette.

"That medicine is generally very rare, and also very expensive," began Chashka before Giorgi interrupted him:

"It can't be more expensive than these," said Giorgi, putting the parcel he had under his arm on the table. He opened it quickly and showed the contents to Chashka. Inside were new, genuine American jeans, which even Chashka was surprised to see. He eyed them for a long time, and then called to Moshe, who was standing in the yard. As soon as he came in, Moshe immediately understood without a word what was going on, and carefully inspected the jeans. Then he looked at Giorgi, smiled smugly, and said to Chashka:

"I swear on my children, they're real Levi's."

Then he turned and looked at Giorgi again. All business, he continued:

"There are loads of clients for them. But you have to tell me the price, buddy, if you leave them with me."

"I need medicine for a child and that's why I'm selling them, and I know nothing about prices at all. It's the first time I'm selling anything," Giorgi said.

Chashka and Moshe looked at each other. Then Chashka turned away, took the medicine out of the cupboard and handed it to Giorgi:

"I'll deduct the price out of the jeans price. Come tomorrow and get the rest of the money from Moshe."

Without another word Giorgi put the medicine in his pocket and said goodbye.

He was sure they'd turn him down for this job too, but he still went by the Research Institute to get the official answer. They apologized to him in the personnel department:

"They have considered your application, but there are no vacancies and probably won't be any until next year. Bring your documents next year and you might get lucky."

"I'll already be very far away next year," Giorgi told the lady wearing red lipstick. He politely took the documents back from her. He put the papers under his arm and, as soon as he was on the street, lit a cigarette. He crossed the street, stopped for a minute on the bridge, calmly threw the documents into the River Mtkvari and continued on his way. He asked a passerby for the time and took a trolley-bus. He had to see the brothers and he knew they would be home at this hour since it was already lunchtime and they always had lunch together at home with the family.

Paata opened the door for him and led Giorgi into the large dining room, where the hosts were sitting around the table. They all stood up to greet Giorgi. He wasn't hungry, but felt he couldn't refuse the father of his friends, so he sat at the table. Even during the meal the father read the *Pravda* newspaper. The elder son quipped to his father with a smile:

"If there were any truth in these newspapers, they surely wouldn't cost five kopeks."

"In Soviet newspapers I only read the news about foreign countries.' Vazha, the father, said. He took off his glasses and smiled at his son but he wouldn't leave his father alone:

"Aren't you interested in the Soviet news?"

"I listen to *Voice of America* for that," Vazha said, still smiling as everyone laughed. "It's easier to determine the truth that way."

For a little while no one broke the silence until Vazha asked:

"Aren't we going to offer a drink to your guest? We don't want him to say afterwards that we gave him a 'dry dinner.'"

"Thanks very much, but I'm in a hurry," Giorgi said and looked at the brothers.

"If you're in a hurry, then we'll drink quickly. How much is for us to decide, right?" Vazha said cheerfully.

"I really have to go," Giorgi said and made a motion to stand up and looked at the brothers again. "I just dropped in to see the boys."

"That's what young people are like nowadays," Vazha said with a smile. "Thank God we don't live in America and you can't buy it here, or else you'd probably be drinking coca-cola, instead of wine."

Still smiling, Vazha shrugged in resignation and got to his feet. Giorgi thanked his hosts once again and followed the brothers into their room.

"I'm ready. I threw my papers into the river today," he said quietly, but convincingly, as he waited for their reaction.

"You must mean into the Mtkvari," Kakhaberber joked, as Paata continued very seriously:

"You've kept your passport, haven't you?"

"I have. And what have you done?"

"What were we supposed to do?"

"You were supposed to see the monk."

"We have."

"And?"

"We haven't told him anything yet. He'll be here in a few days and we'll talk to him."

"Will he agree?"

"We don't know yet."

"We have to get him to agree. We desperately need him. He has to get the weapons into the airplane."

"We know. They'll search the rest of us."

"Last summer when we went to Moscow, there was a priest on our flight and we watched him. He wasn't searched. He was even treated with extra respect for the other passengers to see."

"I know. That's why we need him so much. In any case, I've made up my mind that I'm going. I already know I'll never get a job here."

"What if I did have a job, what's the point? I'll have studied for seventeen years and will be given a hundred and twenty roubles a month, plus deductions."

"I'm off," Giorgi interrupted and stood up. He said goodbye to them both and took out a cigarette: "I'll have it when I go outside."

"At the end of the week we'll know the monk's answer and let you know."

"I'm waiting on you."

Giorgi raised his arm and said goodbye to the brothers once again, and then left.

Manana opened the door for him as Giorgi kissed her. He took the child's medicine out of his pocket.

He handed it to his wife with a satisfied look and sat down on a chair:

"How is he?"

"Asleep."

"Tomorrow I'll have some money too."

"They must have been so happy to offer you the job they're already giving you your first salary tomorrow."

Giorgi smiled.

"They refused me."

"You took the papers?"

Giorgi nodded to Manana.

"Give them to me. I'll put them away. They might be of use someday."

"Where are you going to put them?"

"I'll put them under your Levi's."

Giorgi studied his wife's face carefully, trying to figure out whether she had already found out what happened to his jeans. Unable to read her thoughts, Giorgi replied boldly:

"I don't have the papers anymore."

"Where are they?"

"Probably already in Baku."

Now it was Manana's turn to smile:

"If you threw them into the Mtkvari, your papers haven't even reached Rustavi yet. If you change your mind, you could meet them there."

"I'm not going to change my mind anymore. Everything's already decided."

"What are you going to do about us?"

"I'm going because of you, so I'm not going to leave you here, am I? Let me get out of here first and then, of course, I'll take you too."

"How?"

"I don't know yet."

"But you've decided to go for good?"

"I have."

"You'll probably go wearing those new Levi's."

Manana didn't smile, but for some reason the joke angered Giorgi. He got to his feet, took out a cigarette, lit it, and then put it out again. He left, slamming the door behind him. In his anger, he forgot that the baby was asleep.

On November 18th 1983, just as Giorgi was wounded and received a fatal bullet during the hijack attempt, he probably looked back to the evening he showed his little son a bright star in the sky, telling him to wave at it if he ever missed him...

# THE SEA

The Black Sea was calm and so still that it hardly moved. This was usual in autumn, before the stormy and tempestuous days of winter. At sunset, the sun was big, red and beautiful.

Tina and Gega would watch the sunset from the balcony of the house. There, you could see the entire shoreline, which was thoroughly controlled by Russian border guards with submachine-guns. Turkey was only a couple of villages away. Getting close to the border, even within a few kilometers, was forbidden of course. Tina and Gega rented a room in a house that stood high on a mountain slope with a wonderful balcony. The hosts were Laz and, like most Laz, they often had delicious Black Sea fish to eat. They frequently invited Tina and Gega to lunch and dinner. They became very close to their hosts, but Gega was careful to study English in secret. He did not wish a family that lived so close to the border to find out and grow suspicious.

That's why it was even a bit comical to be learning new words together with Tina in whispers. She covered him in kisses after each correct answer.

On the day before their departure, Tina and Gega took another long walk on the beach and decided to watch the sunset from there, staying late and not hurrying to the house.

The cold of autumn wasn't unbearable just yet. Gega kept close to Tina to keep her warm. She always felt it as they listened to the sound of the sea and waited for the sunset.

Gega put his arm around Tina and kissed her on the cheek. She put her head on his shoulder and once again felt there wasn't anyone else in the entire world closer to her than Gega.

"Can anyone cross the sea swimming?"

"Humans can do anything, if they desire."

"I'm not asking theoretically. Can someone really swim across this sea?"

"In width?"

"Yes, to Turkey.'

"Yes, there was a cameraman or a director at our studio, his last name was Alexandria, and he did it."

"He swam the Black Sea"

"Yes, from here to Turkey."

"How?"

"Slowly..."

"No, seriously."

"He really did it."

"How?"

"He trained and he crossed it."

"All the way?"

"When he got close to Turkey, they picked him up on a ship."

"So he still didn't cross it to the end."

"He didn't need to, he wasn't trying to set a record. He wanted to escape."

"Where is he now?"

"In America..."

Afterwards they sat silently on the beach strewn with white stones, and were utterly surprised when Russian border guards with submachine-guns approached them. At first they demanded IDs and then explained that Tina and Gega were violating a public order with their immoral behaviour. As soon as Tina got to her feet, she looked around to make sure that the deserted beach really wasn't a place for a public gathering. But what shocked her more was that putting your head on your lover's shoulder was apparently immoral behaviour.

Gega grew angry and started talking back to the border guards. With her eyes, Tina begged him not to say anything to them. Gega bit his lip in desperation and complied. He followed her silently and obediently to the house and didn't say anything for a long time.

Gega lay still and Tina stroked his head, very gently, until Gega broke his silence:

"That's why I don't want to live here anymore..."

"The army and police are rude and violent everywhere."

"But love is not forbidden anywhere."

"Not in free countries, I suppose."

"That's what I want. I wish to live in a free country, don't you?"

"I want to be together with you."

"Don't you want freedom?"

"If I'm with you, there's freedom for me anywhere."

"Will you follow me, if I go?"

"I can't swim across the sea."

"Nor can I, I can't swim that well."

"So, what are you going to do?"

"I'm going to fly."

"Are you better at flying?"

"Well, you are an angel. The thing is whether your wings will carry both of us."

"I'm asking you seriously, what are you going to do?"

"I'm also telling you seriously that you are an angel."

"Please be serious."

"I'm really going to fly too, only together with you…" Tina got up, opened the window and looked out at the sea. The Black Sea lived up to its name.

Together with his brothers, Dato listened attentively to Father Tevdore. They were in Dato's room, which seemingly was like that of any other carefree young person.

"After you left, they came up to the monastery again, the very next day."

"What did they want?" asked Paata, taking out a cigarette as he waited for the answer.

"They probably wanted to know what business you had with me."

"And what did you tell them?"

"I told them what we talked about, that time."

"What did we talk about?"

"About God, goodness and love."

"And? Are they scared of those things?"

"That's what scares them most of all, but they won't admit it and won't openly fight with the Church. On the contrary, when people can see it, they treat priests and monks with reverence, but the KGB is secretly watching them all."

"And what are you going to do?"

"The same as I always have been. Obstacles only make my faith stronger. That's how the path of the first Christians began too. Suffering is nourishment for faith"

"You are a monk and you've made your choice."

"People have to make their choices. It doesn't matter whether they are clergymen or laymen. You still have to choose between good and evil, light and darkness, slavery and freedom."

"We've made our choice too," Kakhaberber said, looking at the others and then at the monk, repeating the phrase.

"What choice?" Father Tevdore asked all of them.

The young men looked at each other, as if hesitating. After a short pause Paata looked at Father Tevdore straight in the eyes and calmly said:

"We're going."

"How?"

"On a plane."

"How?"

"We'll land in Turkey, on the American military base, and they'll take care of us from there."

"How?"

"Like refugees. You remember the Brazauskas family, when the Americans received them like heroes?"

"Those Lithuanians were simply lucky."

"We'll be lucky too. We'll scare the pilots a bit to change the flight course."

"How are you going to scare them?"

"With weapons."

"How are you planning to take weapons onto the plane? Everyone is thoroughly searched."

"Except for priests and monks," Dato replied. Together with his friends, he waited for Father Tevdore's reaction.

"What if there are casualties?"

"There won't be."

"What if there are?"

"There won't be."

"The possibility is completely excluded?"

"Nothing can be completely excluded."

"Then there may be."

"Only theoretically."

"It's not worth it, even theoretically."

"What's not worth it?"

"Nothing is worth the life of even one person—neither freedom nor any other goal. Every life belongs only to the Lord, and death is only for the Lord to decide."

"But we're not intending to kill anyone," Paata interrupted as he shot an angry glance at Dato. "We need the weapons only to frighten the pilots, nothing else."

"Fatalities always follow fear. Besides, the pilots won't be allowed to land in Turkey."

"Why not, if the Lithuanians managed to force them?" Paata interrupted him again.

"That's exactly why you won't be able to force them again. The Russian won't repeat that mistake again."

Kakhaberber and Paata stood up, took their jackets, and left without saying goodbye.

Dato and the monk were left alone in the room. After a long pause, Father Tevdore smiled and said:

"They probably thought I was afraid..."

Giorgi met Soso on a crowded street, and was to the point:

"That priest isn't coming."

"I know."

"Only one option remains."

"What option?"

"That girl, Gega's girlfriend, has to take the weapons onto the plane."

"How?"

"Pretend she's pregnant and hide them on her belly."

"She's not even his wife yet."

"He'll marry her first and we can go right after the wedding."

"Is he going to agree?"

"I don't know, but you have to convince him."

"Gega—yes, but Tina?"

"Is her name Tina?"

"Yes, her name's Tina."

"Gega will make her agree. We have no other option. And not much time either," said Giorgi as he left.

Soso stood on the pavement for a little longer, then crossed the street and walked away.

"Has the snow already disappeared?" Dato asked Father Tevdore with surprise, breaking the silence in the monastery yard.

"It's the autumn sun. It's going to snow again in a week."

"It is so quiet here."

"There's peace here and we need more peace than quiet."

"Did you call me here for some peace?"

"No. Why didn't you bring Gega?"

"He's got filming and said he'd definitely come up next week."

"I wanted Gega to be here today too, I wanted to tell you both."

"What?"

"I know you have already decided to go."

"We haven't decided anything yet."

"I'm saying this to you, because I know that if Gega decides to go, you'll follow him."

"They haven't decided anything yet, as I said."

"And I've told you what I feel. And Gega's not coming up here because everything is already decided."

"I told you—no."

"You are free to not tell me anything. That's not the reason I wanted to see you. Quite the opposite. I wanted to tell you what I've already told the others. But they are different, they don't have what the Lord has bestowed upon you."

"And what is that?"

"Common sense. Other languages might not have such an accurate word—when a person's sense and soul guides their actions."

"You know I'm not the one who's making decisions in this case."

"That's why I'm telling you that if you say no and don't go with them, others will also begin to think that even one person's life is more precious than any goal, no matter how great and noble it might be."

"There won't be any fatalities. You believe me, right, that I would never kill anyone? I would rather be a victim myself than for someone else to die. I really would."

"You won't kill. But the special forces will. They will kill their own passengers, innocent people and..."

"And blame us?"

'Of course they will blame you. Worse than that, you really will be responsible for the people they kill."

"Why us?"

"Those people will be killed because of you."

"There will be no victims."

"There will be! You don't know the people who you intend to slap in the face, and Gega probably thinks that it's another play or a film awaiting him to play the part.'

"If several people escape from here, what will this supposed great empire lose?"

"Several...hundreds...thousands, it doesn't mean anything to them. Human life doesn't mean anything to them at all."

"All the more reason to go."

"They won't forgive the insult."

'We're not going to insult anyone.'

"You don't know how evil arrogant people can be when they come to power."

"The same government was unable to do anything about the Lithuanians who hijacked a plane, and let them go."

"That's why they aren't going to repeat that mistake. They won't let you go!"

"We haven't decided anything yet..."

"I know you already have, but if you refuse, someone else will dare to say no too, then another, yet another and all of you will survive. The whole thing will collapse and everyone will survive."

"Nothing is decided yet."

"It'll be too late then. That's why I want to see Gega. He probably thinks that backing down now is a sign of cowardice. I want him to know that it's more important to think about the Lord than about those who want to use him."

"No one can use Gega. No one can force him to do anything he doesn't want to do himself."

"That's exactly the reason I want to see him before it's too late. That's why I'm going to wait for him and reason with him. Tell him I'm waiting."

"I will."

"I'll be waiting for him every day."

"I'll tell him."

When Dato walked down the hill a considerable distance from the monastery, he looked back to where his friend, the monk, was standing at the monastery door. He waved goodbye one last time. Then he turned around and continued and went away...

# THE WEDDING

The wedding looked like a traditional Georgian wedding, but was also totally unlike one. Everything was as it should be, but several people still showed signs of anticipating something extraordinary. They were nervously waiting. For others, it was only the wedding of a happy couple and they enjoyed themselves. Some simply lost themselves in the feast. The bride, whose belly was already showing, looked tired. Gega's mother, with her maternal instinct, could sense something. She didn't know exactly what was going on, but she could clearly feel that the partying, dancing and singing was tainted with sadness.

The behaviour of one guest, Giorgi, seemed especially strange to her. She hadn't met him before. Gega was unable to convince him to join them in the restaurant, so they stood in the entrance talking for quite a long time. Geg's mother Natela, couldn't hear their voices, but she could sense that they were arguing; as if Gega was explaining something to him, but the stranger wouldn't agree with the groom. Giorgi finally left, having never entered the restaurant.

Gega's mother was sure she saw the stranger, who was clearly older than Gega, shake his finger at Gega before he left. Gega then let his head hang down. When he finally returned to the table, he didn't smile for the rest of the party. Natela never knew for sure, neither then nor afterwards, whether she imagined it or whether it all really happened.

The only thing she remembered for certain was to take good care of the guests. There were quite a lot of them, and as a hostess, she was trying to give her share of attention to everyone. She made sure not to neglect anyone. She simply didn't have enough time for her son. But her eyes were in constant search for him. She tried to keep Gega in sight throughout the wedding, especially after the incident with the doves.

It was tradition in Georgia at the time to bring two doves to a wedding and giving them as a symbolic gift to the newlyweds. No one could remember how the two doves appeared at Gega and Tina's wedding. It might have been someone's idea of a joke. When to everyone's delight the doves were set free in the restaurant hall, it was followed by general laugher. But what followed next was beyond anyone's imagination: one of the doves hit the floor as if stricken. In the ensuing silence, someone uttered in a horrified but loud voice:

"One dove is dead."

The dumbfounded wedding guests looked at each other with fear. Some secretly glanced at Tina and Gega. It was Gega who broke the silence and told the musicians which song to play next and the party continued.

The wedding party continued, but everyone felt something very strange and extraordinary had just happened.

The only person who felt that something else, something more important, was still to come, was Gega's mother Natela. She kept searching, constantly searching, for her son. Tired from the wine and noise, Gega sat next to Irakli Charkviani looking sad.

He had his arm around Irakli, whispering to him. Irakli was smiling, though it seemed to Natela that his smile concealed something very important, but she also thought Gega was simply saying goodbye to Irakli. In any case, Gega didn't look like a sentimental drunk proclaiming his love to a friend. Natela didn't know what was really going on and blamed her own curiosity.

Consequently, when Gega was saying goodbye to his friend Dato, Natela didn't pay attention to a packet of cigarettes Gega gave him as a gift. Only afterwards did she remember the conversion they had about the packet of American Camels, which were quite rare in Tbilisi at the time, and Dato's refusal to take them.

"Take them, as a memento from me," said Gega, putting the packet in Dato's pocket.

"I don't want them, I've already got some," said Dato, as he took the cigarettes out of his pocket.

"I'm giving them to you as a memento," Gega repeated with such an expression that Dato smiled and looked at the packet. The packet clearly had "Turkish" printed on it.

"I thought they were American," he said to Gega as he pulled a cigarette out of the packet.

"They are American, they're simply made in Turkey, with Samsun tobacco."

"I know Samsun, there's an American military base there, close to Batumi, only on the other side of the border…"

"Keep it as a memento from me," Gega interrupted him and even seemed embarrassed, but tried not to show it. He hugged Dato for the last time.

It was already very late when the guests left and the tired restaurant staff were slowly clearing the messy tables. The newlyweds' table stood separately, on a dais, and there were only two people sitting in the empty hall—Tina and Gega; left alone after the noisy party. And in this silence Gega whispered to Tina, who looked very, very beautiful:

"We're leaving in the morning."

"I know."

"We've got several hours left."

"I know."

"You've got to make up your mind. We aren't coming back."

"I already have."

"I'm talking about something else."

"I've decided for myself."

"But you didn't want to."

"I still don't want to, but I'm coming."

"Why?"

"Why what? Why I don't want to, or why am I coming?"

"You don't want to, but you're still coming."

"I don't want to, but I'm coming with you."

"Why don't you want to?"

"Because what you intend to do cannot be justified."

"Why?"

"Because anything that might cause human death is unjustifiable."

"There will be no fatalities. We're taking the weapons only to frighten the pilots."

"There are fatalities where there are weapons, and those people who may die have done nothing wrong to us."

"We're going on a small plane. There'll only be a few passengers besides us."

"Even if there is only one, they are innocent."

"If you're scared, it is better to say so now and everything will fall through."

"I'm not scared."

"I still think you're scared, a little bit."

"I'm not scared. Not of flying, or dying. Nor of what you're going to say and are what you're unable to say."

"What do you mean?"

"That I have to take the gun onto the plane."

Tina touched her belly and very carefully, stroked her future child lovingly. Gega was silent for a very long time, but finally asked Tina:

"Why aren't you afraid of anything?"

"Because I'm not afraid of love..."

In the morning Gega was very cheerful. Natela thought he was more delighted about going to his beloved Batumi more than on his honeymoon. After being in noisy Tbilisi and having the wedding party, the late autumn sea and peace and quiet awaited him. The only thing that surprised Natela was Gega's strange farewell?. Gega always used to kiss his mother when leaving home, and then raise his leg in the street, without looking back, for his mother to see from the window.

That morning, she stood at the window, but Gega didn't lift his leg nor did he look back. He just walked away and disappeared...

Amidst the crowded airport, it was hard not to notice the beautiful couple, accompanied by their friends, headed on their honeymoon. The crowds didn't surprise anyone. The newlyweds, however, were surprised by the announcement of the Batumi flight. Instead of a small plane which, as a rule flew between Tbilisi and Batumi, that morning, for some reason the flight was with a large airplane flying to Batumi and then continuing to Leningrad. Such a change startled several passengers so much that their faces clearly showed hesitation. Finally, considering it was only an unlucky coincidence, they went through ticket and passport control like the rest of the travelers. The only person who didn't go through the regular registration was the pregnant Tina, for whom it was already dangerous to pass through the magnetic arch because of the radiation. The airport employees complied with Gega's request with pleasure, even congratulating Gega and Tina on their marriage. Then someone opened a bottle of sparkling wine and those with a hangover drank with obvious enthusiasm and toasted the newlyweds several times with such fervour that they almost missed the flight. Finally, everyone took their seats in the plane and the flight attendant explained the safety rules to the careless passengers, who never listened to flight attendants.

Then they took off...

However, there was an unplanned disturbance before the flight, which caused a delay. An extremely drunk passenger was out of control and the crew had to call the police. As a result, passenger 59 was marched off the plane.

What the fifty-ninth passenger didn't know was that very soon after takeoff, the remaining fifty-eight passengers would be envious of him.

It was already noon, but Natela was asleep because she had been cleaning the house all night. In the morning she saw her son and daughter-in-law off to their honeymoon and set to wash the dishes, but she was very sleepy. She was so tired she even found it hard to remain standing, so she left the dishes. Deciding she'd take a short nap, she made herself comfortable in an armchair on the balcony. Though quite drowsy, Natela was never able to say afterwards whether she was really asleep, or simply had her eyes closed, when there was a timid knock on the window. It was right next to her and the first thing she felt was fear.

At first she was simply frightened, since there was a bearded man with extremely expressive green eyes, standing under the window in clerical garb.

"Hello," said the monk, apologizing to Natela for disturbing her.

"Hello," said Natela. She had no idea what business this monk or priest could have with her.

"Gega lives here, right?" the stranger asked.

She calmed down a bit at the mention of her son's name. "Yes."

"If he's in, could I see him for a minute?"

"Gega isn't here. They left today."

"Where to?"

"They're on their honeymoon."

"You must be his mother."

"I am."

"Where have they gone?"

"To Batumi."

"Can I ask how they went?"

"Excuse me, but who are you?"

"I am Gega's spiritual father."

"I didn't know my son had a confessor."

"Gega didn't know himself."

"Sorry, but I don't think I follow."

"I am his friends' spiritual father and I have been waiting for Gega as well."

"Where have you been waiting?"

"At my monastery. I've waited for days but when he didn't show up, I came myself."

"He'll probably call today, so could I take a message?"

"How did they go?"

"By plane."

"Have they departed already?"

"They must be in the air already." Automatically, Natela looked at the clock on the wall. "About an hour ago."

"Did the others go with them?"

"Yes, the boys went with them."

"I was supposed to go too, but I was late."

"Did they know you were also going?"

"They didn't. Nor did I."

"I'm afraid I don't understand you."

"I am their spiritual father and should be together with them now on that plane."

"Did you miss the flight?"

"I didn't know they were going today."

"But you wanted to go with them."

"I didn't want to go at all and I didn't want them to go, either."

"I apologize again, but I still don't understand you."

"I don't understand either why they hurried..."

Natela didn't say anything else to the monk, though she still didn't understand what he meant. Suddenly she realized while she had been talking to the visitor from the window it was getting cold.

"Come in, please." Only now did Natela invite him in and the monk smiled.

"Thank you very much, but I must be going. It's already late. Everything is late."

"What shall I tell Gega when he calls?"

"Where from?"

"From Batumi," Natela said, the anger mounting in her.

"If he calls, tell him I'm praying for them and will always be praying for them."

The monk turned to go, then looked back and said good-bye to her as he left.

Only then did Natela begin to wonder why the monk knocked on the window and not on the door and, unable to find an explanation, she went over his words. In her anxiety, her thoughts flowed in one direction and then the next. She called the families of Gega's friends to find out whether they knew anything. She called the homes of those who she knew for sure were together with Gega and Tina, but she received the same answer everywhere—no one had called from Batumi yet, which meant the plane was still in the air.

Then Natela really fell asleep, utterly exhausted. She fell into a very deep sleep and slept until the evening. She slept, until they woke her up...

Tina Petviashvili, Gega Kobakhidze

"The Monk," Father Tevdore Chikhladze

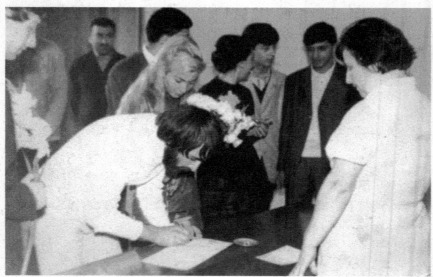

Temur Chikhladze (before he became Father Tevdore) and
Guliko Eristavi's wedding ceremony

Gega Kobakhidze

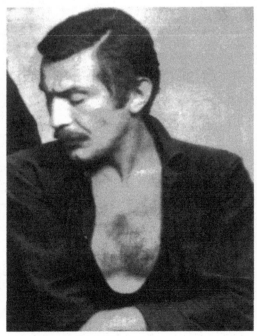

Among the hijackers was aspiring
painter Gia Tabidze

Kakhaber Iverieli, Paata Iverieli, Unknown

Gega Kobakhidze, Irakli Charkviani,
Giorgi Mirzashvili

Soso Tsereteli, Dato Mikaberidze,
Gia Tabidze

"The Monk," Father Tevdore Chikhladze

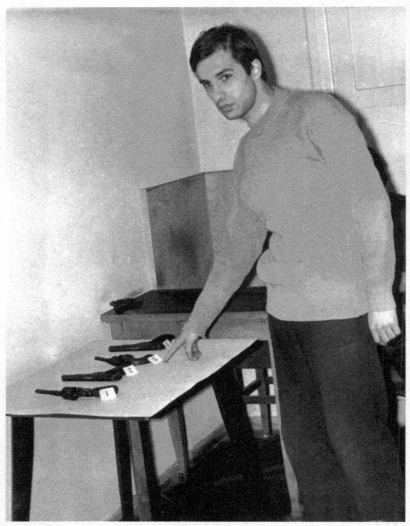

Identifying evidence from the failed hijacking during the governmental investigation

# THE PLANE

Later referred to as a hijack, it looked more like a group suicide of the desperate.

The hijackers were dressed casually, just like the jeans generation did in those days. Only Giorgi Tabatadze wore a suit with a tie and held a globe in his arms. He also had the Bible, which he passed to Gega once on board. Later, the globe disappeared, later giving birth to an assumption that the guns were smuggled inside it. In reality, Tina's friend had them in her handbag without knowing it.

Giorgi took only a globe and the Georgian Bible. He left behind an amazing letter for his son, in which he told little Giorgi how to find the shining star whenever he missed his father.

After delays from the unruly drunk, there were problems with weather once they were in the air. According to the official report, when approaching Batumi, the pilots received information about worsening weather conditions

and changed the course. Some theorized that such a sudden change likely seemed suspicious to the hijackers and
so they acted immediately. However, based on the black
box data, the official report also mentioned that the pilots
weren't receiving orders from the flight dispatchers, but
from military authorities, which lends credence to the like-
lihood there was a pre-planned operation.

Among the fifty-eight passengers on the plane, there was
one who didn't have any business in Batumi whatsoever.
His job was to sit on the plane, just as KGB officers accompanied other flights. In Soviet airspace, there was not a single flight without at least one KGB officer traveling under
the guise of a regular passenger. All Soviet citizens were
aware of it, as were Gega's friends. In their attempt to hijack
the plane, they were convinced that they had to identify
the KGB agent accompanying their flight right away. They
thought that getting rid of him would make it considerably
easier to force the crew to cross the border from Batumi
and land in Turkey at one of the US military bases. However, they didn't know for certain which of the fifty-eight
passengers was the KGB officer, so their plans were only
speculative. It was like a childhood game where kids identified spies based on their clothes. Accordingly, they decided
that a middle-aged man sitting in the first row was the
agent because he wore a grey raincoat. Though Gega voiced
his uncertainty, most of the conspirators had a different
opinion supported by a "very solid" argument mentioned by
one of them and then repeated by the rest.

"That's him for sure, look at his typical KGB face!"

"Yes, he does look like one, but what if he's an ordinary
passenger?" Gega's question had little effect on the others.

"If that's not him, then search for someone else, show
him to me and I'll take care of him," Kakhaberber advised
Gega, as Giorgi laughed.

"Where am I supposed to look for one?" Gega was genuinely surprised.

"Here, on the airplane," said Giorgi. It became clear to Gega that the choice had already been made.

Acting quicker than Kakhaber, Giorgi got to his feet and headed towards the cockpit with a bottle of sparkling wine in his hand that he drained on the way. When he approached the first row, he hit the selected passenger on his head with the bottle, catching him completely unawares, and the attempt to hijack the plane began.

Much later, only when everything was over, did it transpire that the hijackers were wrong. The middle-aged man, who passed out right away from the blow, was actually an ordinary passenger, not a KGB agent. However, it didn't make any difference to the man at the time, since he lay sagging in his seat, with a gash on his head, while a woman sitting next to him screamed loudly with fear and shock for the whole plane to hear.

It was strange that the racket didn't cause a panic among the hijackers at all. It seems they were prepared for the reaction, so they began to carry out their plan without delay.

As soon as Giorgi had got up from his seat with the bottle in his hand, the others immediately took their positions and the first with a weapon in his hand to reach the pilots was Giorgi himself, who was closely followed by his elder brother. But Giorgi didn't even have time to pass their demands to the crew in the cockpit. Without any warning, an armed man shot Giorgi, killing him on the spot. The armed man in plain clothes was sitting facing the aisle and with his back to the sky. His presence in the cockpit was completely unexpected to the hijackers.

They had studied plans for a small plane, and this larger one was all new to them. The cockpit of a small plane didn't have enough space for anyone apart from the pilots. No one

could fit there as comfortably as that armed man who surprised Giorgi and Kakhaber.

Giorgi was dead and the hijackers didn't have time to think
about their mistakes. There was no time left for thinking at
all, since the armed man was already shooting down the aisle.
Fifty something passengers sitting on the plane ducked their
heads at the sound of the gun. So did the hijackers, but bullets
can never distinguish between the guilty and the innocent. The
shooter had little time to think either. He wounded Kakhaberber, and another passenger, which led the flight attendant,
possibly instinctively, to close the cockpit door. She may have
closed the door in order to block the way for the hijackers, so
they couldn't reach the pilots. Regardless, it proved difficult
due to the first victim lying motionless in the entrance.

The others, despite the general panic and the unsuccessful and tragic beginning, still tried to carry out what they
had intended. There was simply nothing else left for them
to do now. The others had guns, while Gega was standing
in the aisle with a hand grenade in his hand. It was a fake,
but only Giorgi knew it and he was already dead.

Gega threatened to pull the pin unless the crew flew the
plane to Turkey. But the pilots had already received orders
from the ground to not comply with any of the demands of
the hijackers.

Then, In order to disorganize the hijackers, the pilots
sent the plane into a freefall. It was completely unnecessary, since the hijackers were already acting completely
chaotic anyways and such a freefall harmed the innocent
passengers most of all. The fall was so severe and unexpected that the passengers were thrown from their seats,
with blood-curdling screams. What was most horrifying,
was that the pilots repeated the maneuver several times.

When the plane had finally settled down, the hijackers
repeated their demand, more categorically this time. The

violence and unexpected turn of events had made them desperate. Meanwhile, the pilots were forced to come up with a lie in order to gain some time and calm them down, at least temporarily. They told Soso that there was enough fuel to reach Batumi and that they simply wouldn't be able to reach any airport in Turkey. This sounded suspicious to Soso, as it would to any other hijacker, but they were forced to believe the pilots and agreed to fill the fuel tanks at Sokhumi. Sokhumi airport was the closest to Batumi and it seemed the only way out of this situation. In truth, the pilots had received orders to return to Tbilisi, since it was at Tbilisi airport that a Russian armed unit, based near the airport, was already waiting for the hijackers. In order to deceive the hijackers further, the pilots performed a maneuver to make it appear they had changed course and were flying to Sokhumi. It was unnecessary since nobody had any idea of the technicalities of flying a plane. The hijackers weren't even able to find out, until the end, whether two fighter jets were really following their airplane in case they headed to Turkey. If an escort really did appear in the sky near Batumi, it was more to influence the pilots to follow orders or else face the plane being brought down as soon as it got close to the Turkish border.

The hijackers realized the true destination of the flight only when the contours of the city appeared and the plane began to land. That was exactly when Dato decided everything was over; that it made no sense to try to justify oneself. He killed himself as soon as he became convinced the plane had landed at Tbilisi's airport again.

The sound of his gunfire broke the silence that had temporarily settled on the plane. Passengers, sitting near Dato instinctively cried out. None of them could have imagined the horror that still awaited them.

When they landed, many of the passengers thought they had survived, but the minute the plane stopped, several dozen armed soldiers surrounded it and, without any warnings or ultimatums, opened fire on the plane. It was unclear who gave the order to launch the assualt. In any case, it was difficult to imagine what the intention was for Soviet soldiers to fire at the plane from the outside.

When the nightmare finally ended, only the moans of the wounded could be heard on the plane, while those still unharmed were simply silent with shock, unable to utter a sound.

Soso's silence was due to a wound in his throat. It was hard for him to speak, but he still noticed the air hostesses openeing the emergency locks. Their eyes asked him if the passengers could leave, and he nodded in consent. The attendants believed it was the only way of escape under the circumstances, but the passengers received a volley of gunfire as soon as they emerged from the plane. Surprisingly unscathed, Irina Khomich showed amazing resolve when she later refused to change her testimony about what she had seen. She recalled that the Soviet soldiers shot not only at those passengers and crew members jumping from the plane, but at the remaining passengers as well.

It was specifically for this reason that the hijackers yelled at the passengers to put their open palms against the portholes in hope of halting the shooting squad. Alas, the desperate attempt only resulted in most passengers being wounded in their palms.

After landing in Tbilisi airport, Paata was the most composed, and even tried to encourage the others. He might have been pushed to action because his wounded brother pleaded to stop his suffering and shoot him. Incidentally, Soso had also asked Paata to kill him as soon as the squad began to fire. Paata was wounded in his leg, but still had enough strength to move around. Later, the witness accounts proved that some passengers helped him bandage his leg—one lady even tore her dress to wrap the wound. Paata moved around the plane until nearly the very end, yelling when the shooting started. He was reported to have told the passengers that they—the hijackers—knew they were dying for freedom, but the rest were about to perish for nothing...

In his subsequent testimony, Paata Iverieli explained that his loud and aggressive behaviour was due to fear. He worried that any signs of softness would have resulted in passengers attacking him and his friends before the plane was stormed. He also believed he had to demonstrate aggression in order to convince the authorities that the hijackers were serious and not a bunch of romantic students.

Unlike the rest of the group, Paata still thought that it was not over. He hoped they could demand fuel, get the dead and wounded off the plane and fly to Turkey. As soon as the officials approached the bullet-riddled plane and began negotiations, the hijackers gave them their ultimatum.

Yet in actuality, the negotiations were only a means for the authorities to gain time. They had no intention of satisfying the hijackers' demands. They played for time. A special task force unit was on its way from Russia. The unit was specially activated for operations against armed terrorists. Until they arrived, the local government even tried to use the hijackers' parents in order to negotiate.

Their parents were brought to the airport, but for some reason the authorities changed their mind. They believed that these supposed misguided young people would listen more to the First Secretary of the Central Committee rather than to their own parents. And so, the First Secretary addressed the hijackers, urging them to drop their weapons and turn themselves in.

The address turned fatal for Soso, who stood in the open door of the plane and gathered his remaining strength to swear at the First Secretary. Later, when everything was over, the general opinion was that it was this insult that resulted in no surgeon being allowed near him. Soso would ultimately die from blood loss hours later.

By then, the others still on the plane were losing blood too. However the wounded were not taken away by ambulance despite the categorical demands of the hijackers. The hijackers thought this was a true demonstration of the Soviet authorities' cold-bloodedness and were shocked at the lack of compassion for innocent citizens. But the authorities calculated that the more wounded people there were on the airplane, the better it was for them, because their panic and agony would prevent the hijackers from thinking logically.

Fourteen hours after the plane landed, an operation to free those onboard started. Several managed to jump from the plane, probably with consent of the hijackers. Tina's two friends were allowed to leave the plane, and Tina and Gega were encouraged to give up. Naively, the hijackers sent some passengers to negotiate with the authorities. Those released never went back. The hijackers believed it was a misunderstanding, and sent more passengers to the officials. There was little hope in negotiations, but they had no alternative. Sooner or later they would have to face the truth, to realize they were being deceived. They should have realized it when they released one of the passengers with a threat that if he did not return they would shoot his brother who was still on board. The passenger never returned.

The only official who negotiated with the hijackers was an airport employee, though it was just another ploy for time. He found ridiculous excuses for the hijackers, but they believed him. He claimed that Turkey refused to receive the plane but that Iran agreed on condition the petrol tank was filled to the brim. Instead, the hijackers demanded to go to Israel, and ordered that the ground crew fill the plane's tank in only their underwear.

As this went on, the special task force had arrived from Russia and were lying on the roof of the plane, waiting for the orders to start the operation. They impatiently waited for their commanders' order as it continually rained.

They received the order to go ahead only after Tina, with a grenade in her hand, appeared in the plane hatch. She'd asked Gega for the grenade.

"It's not real," he told her, so weak he was unable to smile anymore.

"I know," said Tina, kissing Gega as she took the grenade and headed for the hatch.

Seeing a girl with a grenade, the authorities decided it was time to act and their operation was over in seven minutes. They let gas off inside the plane and then simply threw both the hijackers and the remaining passengers out onto the ground. They were taken to the airport, where government officials and KGB generals waited. A high-ranking official kicked Soso. He fell to the ground and was kicked again for the First Secretary to see. It was too good a chance for him to miss.

It was still raining in Tbilisi and word had reached the Georgian capital that the students had failed to hijack the airplane.

# THE RENDEZVOUS

Opinions in Tbilisi and the rest of country were divided over what happened. Many people were deeply shocked, even though no one was sure of the details. The media and the authorities immediately started a campaign to push public opinion in their favour. Before a full investigation began, the government set out to present the plane hijackers as monsters and bandits. It was a necessary step, as there was a strong anti-Soviet mood at that time and some voices began to defend and justify the actions of the hijackers. To shift opinion, the government unleashed a propaganda campaign on television. It also resorted to old Bolshevik methods: staff meetings were held in all institutions and organizations, where workers and employees denounced the incident and adopted resolutions demanding severe punishment for the traitors. The intent was to make the impending harsh verdict appear as the will of the people and not the authorities. Few imagined the court would be as ruthless as they were, but others were aware that the government would not be lenient in order to make an example of the hijackers and send a message.

There was little attempt by investigators to collect evidence in the case. The Soviet court was only interested in a decision, not facts or arguments. But still, certain issues had to be discussed. For instance, the Central Committee spent a long time looking into who was to be blamed for being the head of this terrorist group. Several options were investigated, including the hijackers' parents. But their final choice proved best suited for their goals. The monk, Father Tevdore, was charged with being the head of the gang and was arrested two weeks after the hijack attempt. The fact that he even wasn't even there for the incident didn't mean anything to the investigation and the government. The main thing for the government was that a monk, a representative of the Church, would be declared as the head of the plot at the court hearing. They could then use the hearing to clearly demonstrate to the public how anyone's interest in religion ends.

From the day of the unsuccessful hijacking, Tevdore had zealously prayed for those who perished and those who survived. He never thought of hiding. When he was arrested, the KGB and the police found him at the snow-covered monastery.

"You are under arrest!" they told the monk.

He only smiled at the words. One of the eager KGB men decided that the smile was an insult. So he rigorously addressed the smiling monk for the others to hear:

"What are you laughing at?"

Father Tevdore didn't reply, but pointed, with his right hand at one of the monastery rooms. "I've got books and my belongings in there. I'll take them."

"You aren't going to need them," advised another officer.

As he was taken through the monastery yard, the monk thought back to the last day he saw Dato. He now had his friend constantly in his prayers...

The monk was taken directly to the KGB jail and immediately interrogated. The room with the waiting investigator was in the lowest part of the building, so they made Father Tevdore walk for a very long time through long, underground corridors. As soon as he was brought into the room he felt fatigued.

At first, he wondered if the man inside was an investigator at all. The man's first words weren't like those of an investigator's question.

"Those bastards probably hurt your feelings the most."

"Sorry, but I don't understand you."

"I don't understand leaving the organizer out of it, either."

"I was never their leader, I was their confessor."

"What difference does it make whether you were their confessor or personal priest, if they've named you as their leader?"

"Astonishing."

"That's exactly what surprises me. How could they deliberately leave you, the boss, out of it?"

"Sorry, but I really don't understand you."

"I've already told you, I don't get it either. What's the point in leaving the leader behind? You put a lot of effort into it, prepared everything and when at the end, those bastards decided to go without you."

"I never intended to go anywhere."

"That doesn't matter. The bastards should've told you something, you were still the mastermind behind the gang."

"I am a monk."

"That's what I am telling you too, that you are a monk and they cheated you. That's why they really have to answer before you, to say the least."

"I don't know what you're talking about."

"You've got to demand an answer from them. They've wronged you, in every way."

"I already told you, I didn't intend to go anywhere and they knew it perfectly well. Besides, why should they have told me when they were going to fly?"

"Come on, when you do something for which you may be executed, you should at least keep a plan, no?"

"Whose execution do you mean?"

"Everybody who deserves to be shot."

"They didn't kill anyone."

"They slaughtered half of the plane, so many innocent passengers are dead."

"But they haven't killed anyone."

"Did I kill those people, then?"

"I didn't say that, but you know that they didn't shoot at the passengers."

"Are you dumb or what? You sent them on this mission. You should at least know what they've done."

"I didn't send anyone anywhere. I was, and am, categorically against any kind of violence."

"The hijacking was planned at your monastery and we have plenty of evidence to prove it."

"Impossible."

"We also thought it impossible that you'd plan such a thing, especially at a monastery. Maybe you're going to say they never came to see you there, either?"

"I don't deny that. They often came to my monastery."

"Then why did they come to see you at such a distance, aren't there enough churches in Tbilisi?"

"With the Lord's blessing, there are many in Tbilisi, but they needed a spiritual father, like many of us do."

"What does a spiritual father mean? Someone who plans airplane hijackings?"

"A spiritual father is a person who assists another person in searching for the truth."

"That's some truth you helped them find. They'll be probably mentioning you a lot, just before they face the firing squad."

"But they haven't killed any passengers, there has been no trial or verdict yet, and you..."

"They've already passed a verdict for themselves. You know when? Back when they went up the gangway to that airplane."

"I wasn't on that plane at all."

"That doesn't matter. You taught and sent them on their mission, while they left you out of it without even telling you when they were going."

"I didn't want to go."

"This makes your crime even more severe. So, you didn't want to go but sent others to their deaths?"

"I haven't sent anyone anywhere."

"I don't know, but everyone's pointing at you as the gang leader."

"I don't believe you."

"We didn't believe it either, that a monk could plan to hijack a plane. But hey, here you are, aren't you?"

"You want to blame me for being the gang leader?"

"We want you to admit what a harmful influence the Church can have on youth. We don't have many young people to lose."

"But if their fate is already decided, and if they are still going to be executed, what need is there for my confession?"

"That's the thing. You seem quite smart and can figure out that if you take the blame, they may escape execution. How old are you?"

"I am thirty-three today."

Unexpectedly, the investigator stood up and hugged Father Tevdore, congratulating him on his birthday.

"Isn't that better? Think, you aren't a boy anymore."

The monk got to his feet and was accompanied to his cell by the same guard who had brought him to the interrogation room an hour earlier.

In Moscow, there was still distrust of the Georgian authorities, so a special commission was sent to Tbilisi in order to investigate the hijackers' case. The Kremlin suspected the Georgian government would spare the students and the investigation would not be satisfactory with their wishes. Though the local authorities were ultimately harsh in punishing the accused, the Russians still sent a special investigation group to Tbilisi. At the time, any high-raking commission from Moscow was invariably treated as a special guest. Russians always loved Georgian cuisine, wine and brandy and their local hosts always lived up to expectations. Their hosts made them drink and drink, and after excessive drink, they were taken to their beds—asleep, tired and miserable.

During his interrogation, Gega was surprised to be interrogated by two people. One was the familiar old Georgian investigator he was used to, but the other was a new Russian investigator.

With a smile, the Georgian investigator casually offered water to Gega. When he refused, the investigator moved on to business straightaway.

"I'm listening," said Gega. He hated the interrogation process but was still glad each time they took him to be questioned, because he hoped to see Tina, or one of the others, maybe by accident, somewhere in the passage.

The investigation continued for nine months and during this time the plane hijackers were interrogated almost daily. None of them saw each other. None of them were permitted to see their family members even once. They were totally isolated so that none of them knew anything about the others until the trial.

There was, however, an exception on the day Gega met these two investigators. As was the rule, Gega was ordered to face the wall before entering the room. He didn't need to be reminded, since he had already been to the interrogation so many times. This time, he instinctively put his hands on his back and stood facing the wall.

And suddenly, on that wall above his head, he saw a lyric of the English song that he and Tina used to listen to when they were together. There were two English words from that very song scribbled on the wall—*wish you.*

Gega didn't remember whether these words were from that song's title or chorus, but he remembered that the phrase definitely was from that song. It was written on the wall in such small letters, in such hurried handwriting, that he came to only one possible conclusion: if the author of the inscription was Tina as he guessed, then he had to write the ending of the phrase, right there, on the same wall. Then he would get an answer. He was so overjoyed that he couldn't even follow what the investigators were saying. He could think of only one thing—how to steal a pen from the investigator's desk, which he needed now like never before.

Gega sat in the investigator's room, but his mind remained outside, at that corridor wall. For the first time since his arrest, he felt happiness, or something close to it.

The Georgian investigator was surprised by the strange excitement of the prisoner.

"You seem happy today."

"Happy?"

"If not happy, at least pleased."

"What should I be pleased about?"

"That's what surprises me."

"It must be a false impression."

"We never get false impressions. You are the one who was under the false impression thinking you were starring in a movie on that plane as you held a grenade in your hand."

"I've already told you I sincerely regret what happened and that the hand grenade wasn't even real."

"Did you kill all those people with toy weapons, then?"

"We didn't kill anyone."

"Did they commit suicide then?"

"Only Dato committed suicide."

"We've already talked about this. I believe, you were supposed to think it over."

"What was I supposed to think over?"

"You had to decide who was the gang leader."

"As I've said earlier, we didn't have any leader."

"Every gang has a leader."

"We didn't."

"I understand that you don't want to turn into an informer, but it's necessary for the court that you name someone."

"Who am I supposed to name?"

"Your leader. Two of you are dead, you can name one of them."

"How can I do that to a friend?"

"The dead don't mind."

"But I will know I'm lying. We didn't have any leader."

"Then who was that monk?"

"He was a monk."

"Was he a monk or the gang leader?"

"If he had been the leader, he would have been on that plane."

"Just between the two of us, that was a nasty thing to do. The man helped you with everything and then you got rid of him. I've never heard of leaving the leader out of the events."

"He knew nothing."

"You can say that to him," said Georgian investigator, referring to his Russian counterpart, though not pointing to him. "But you don't need that kind of talk with me.

I'm asking you off the record and you should also understand me. How can that be? The man encouraged you and then he wasn't even on the plane. Why should you all be responsible?"

"The monk knew nothing," Gega repeated with indifference.

It did not matter whether this young Georgian investigator believed him or not. Gega's thoughts were firmly glued to the wall, right by the door, where those two English words were written.

"I'm trying for your own sake, so think," the young investigator preached to the prisoner once again as he stood up.

Gega was glad that the day's interrogation was over so soon. Besides, he already had the only pen.

Once outside the interrogation room, when the guard ordered him to face the wall, Gega somehow managed to add two more words under Tina's writing: *were here*.

As the guards took him down the long passage to his cell, Gega thought ahead to the day they would take him for interrogation again. He desperately wanted to see the inscription on the wall. New words would appear underneath if Tina had really written that phrase.

Gega was sleepless that night. He had many sleepless nights before, but this time it was because he had something to look forward to.

At dawn, he somehow managed to stop thinking about Tina and went to sleep, but was awoken once again as he thought back to his investigator. He couldn't understand why they had replaced his first investigator, or how they could assign such a young, inexperienced investigator to the case. It may have been done purposefully, because an investigator that was roughly the same age as Gega might find it easier to find commonality with him more and make him confess. Gega had nothing to tell, or rather, had nothing to hide. Everything really happened as it did. Yet, that night Gega started to wonder if maybe investigations worked as badly as everything else in the Soviet Union...

# THE BROTHERS

Among the prisoners, the most stubborn was Paata. Generally, he did not answer the investigator's questions. If forced, he would only give a few general words. He had survived by sheer accident when he was dragged out of the plane by the special forces. The plane was still under heavy fire when he was taken out in handcuffs. The special forces believed it was their professional duty to protect him and shielded him from the gunfire with their bodies.

Pata was a shooting target as he was brought down the gangway, and he later sat in his cell and contemplated why the authorities had sentenced him to death at the airport. He suspected that he was mistakenly taken for his brother Kakhaber, who was the only survivor who had managed to get into the cockpit. Kakhaber would have known the truth, which was extremely dangerous for the authorities. Paata also thought the KGB was determined to kill him on the gangway because the released passengers described him as the most vicious of the hijackers. There might have been other reasons, but the fact was that he was handcuffed and unarmed, and they wanted him dead.

Had he known for sure that he was the one being shot at instead of his brother, Paata would not have felt so bitter. The brothers adored each other. The plan to leave the USSR and hijack a plane was postponed by Kakhaber, who flatly refused to leave without his younger brother.

Unlike Gega, Paata was interrogated by an experienced elderly investigator who wrote down his meaningless answers each time.

Then, one day Paata unexpectedly faced off with a completely different, young investigator and he began to feel a pain in his stomach. The investigator addressed him with a friendly smile and offered him a cigarette. Paata lit it without a word. The investigator broke the silence.

"We live in the same district."

"I don't remember you."

"Not surprising. You and your brother studied in Moscow, while I graduated from Vladivostok."

"We probably went to the same kindergarten," Paata said with a smile.

"We're from the same district and might have gone to the same kindergarten. I remember for sure there were brothers in my group."

"I didn't go to kindergarten. I hated onions in my soup."

"What about your brother?"

"Nor did he. My brother didn't like mashed potatoes."

"I saw him the other day, but he didn't mention mashed potatoes."

"Do you see him often?"

"When I want to. When it's necessary."

"How is he?"

"He's alright for a prisoner. I try to pay more attention to him, you know, being from the same district."

"Is he in this building too?"

"I told you, he's alright."

In truth, Paata hadn't the slightest idea which building he was kept in, but he strongly suspected he was in the KGB prison along with other political prisoners. The building was off Rustaveli Avenue, behind the central post office. Nothing in its facade revealed its true function because the cells were in the underground maze of multi-tiered passages.

"When will you see him?" Paata asked, though he didn't expect a truthful answer.

"Do you want me to take a message?"

"Will you?"

"I'll tell him whatever you want."

"Tell him I am alright, nothing else."

"Nothing else?"

"No."

"Don't be shy about it. If you want to tell him something, I'll pass it on to him."

"I told you, nothing else."

"If you want to say something to your brother before the trial, or warn him, you know what I mean. I'm telling you this between us."

"Tell him what I told you, nothing else."

"I mean, it's better for you guys if it doesn't turn out at the trial that one says one thing and the other something else, you know ..."

"No one can say anything new at the trial. As it is, everyone knows what really happened."

"Yeah, that was the general belief, but now it turns out some monk was your leader."

"What monk?"

"Father Tevdore."

"Where did you get that from?"

"He has admitted it himself."

"Under torture?"

"Come on, how can you say that? What good would torture do anyway? He'd say one thing now and then have second thoughts at the trial. We don't want that at all."

"Then how did he confess if he wasn't even on the plane and knew nothing?"

"That's what surprises me too. I'm baffled. You know what else surprises me? Now, strictly between you and I, how could he stay at the monastery and let you go to be butchered?"

"He knew nothing about the plane."

"Because you hadn't told him, that's why."

"Even if we had, he would have been against it."

"I don't know, he's saying very different things now."

"Like what?"

"He says he was the organizer. Who would take such blame for nothing?"

"He's lying."

"Why would he do that?"

"He wants to save us."

"Then he really was the organizer."

"That monk has no connection with our case. He wasn't even on the plane."

"He says he planned everything, but ..."

"But what?"

"If at least one person confirms that at the trial..."

"You won't be able to find such a person, because he was absolutely against hijacking the plane."

"But didn't you say, just now, he hadn't known anything about it? I'm telling you this, because we're from the same district and I want to help you. I'll still be living and walking down our district streets, I've got kids growing

up, so I'd like to look people in the eyes. You know what
I mean."

"The monk had nothing to do with this and I can't help
you with anything."

"Help yourself man, no one's telling you to help us."

"I'll be going."

"Go then, and think. I'm right here and I'll help you with
everything. Besides, we're close to each other. It's my duty
in a way, so if you need anything, don't be shy about it."

"What could I need?"

"I don't know, but we're men and there's stuff to worry
about, things to think about. I'm sometimes so tired myself,
it's really hard for me unless I take something to help me.
You know? My job here, family there, so many problems
and things to worry about. No one can say I am a drug
addict, but sometimes one can't deal with it all without a
little help."

"I don't need anything."

"I know, it's just that your doctor told me you've got some
kind of pain and I thought I could find something like a
painkiller for you."

"I don't need anything."

"As you wish. I am just trying to be helpful, being kind
of close to you."

"I don't need anything."

Paata stood up, smiled and the investigator called the
guard. When they were taking him out of the room, the
investigator was still talking to him, but Paata wasn't listening anymore, instead he concentrated on his pain.

It had bothered him since dinner yesterday, if what they
fed him could be called dinner. But Paata was thinking
about something else. He was wondering how the investigator could have known about his aches if Paata hadn't mentioned it to anyone. Once in the cell, he decided to ask to see

a physician. As expected, he had no painkillers, especially for this particular pain...

When they told Gega he was being taken for questioning again, he looked so delighted that the guard was genuinely surprised. He strode down the passage so hurriedly that the guard even reprimanded him several times, but Gega only thought of the wall where Tina's answer was waiting for him at the interrogation room. When they ordered him to stand at that wall, his heartbeat quickened just like back on their first date.

Next to the two English words he had written several days ago, there were small, but legible, letters beginning the exact verse from *The Knight In The Panther's Skin* that Tina had once read aloud to Gega: "Here I sit in prison." Gega, right then, quickly inscribed the continuation "so tall..."

At the interrogation, he didn't listen at all to the investigator, who had been replaced again, and was quite elderly this time. He found himself thinking of the night when they were at the seaside house and Tina had taken *The Knight in The Panther's Skin* from a bookshelf.

They were lying very close to the window, where they could look out at the sea, and that night the moon was so big and bright they didn't even need to light a candle to read. It had been Tina's idea:

"I'll open *The Knight in The Panther's Skin* with my eyes closed, and read out whatever passage I happen to see. Then you'll do the same, put your finger on one of the pages and read."

Now, in the interrogation room, Gega clearly remembered that Tina had come upon exactly this line the very first time she opened the book: "Here I sit in prison so tall..."

The investigator, meanwhile, wondered why this prisoner charged with the gravest crime, and facing the death penalty, had such a happy face. He was totally unaware it was the happiest day for Gega because he was finally convinced that Tina was alive. She was well, and most importantly she wasn't alone. There were the two of them: Tina and their unborn baby. Gega didn't know exactly which cell his wife and their unborn child were in, but the main thing for him was that they were alive. During questioning, he only thought about when it would end, hoping he would have enough time to write a few more words on that wall: *our baby* or *hello to the little one* or *take care of the baby*...

Gega thought about Tina stroking her belly, how her beautiful fingers touched where a new human was already growing...

Meanwhile, the investigator welcomed the prisoner's unusually good mood, as he couldn't have asked for a better moment to tell Gega the news.

"At the trial, you have to confirm that the airplane hijacking was arranged by the monk."

"Why?"

"Because he was the real organizer of the hijacking."

"I've already told the investigation that it is absurd. It is impossible for a person to lead something which he categorically opposes."

"The investigation knows everything and it's already proven with solid evidence that he was the organizer. The monk himself also says he directed everything."

"Then what do you want from me?"

"It's necessary for one of you to confirm the same at the hearing."

"Why me? I didn't know him at all."

"That doesn't matter to us. The main thing is for one of you to confirm that it was precisely the monk who was the organizer and it's easiest for you to do it."

"Why me?"

"Because your wife is expecting a baby and, according to the Soviet law, a pregnant woman cannot be imprisoned."

"You've never observed the law, so why start now?"

"We've always observed the law and will observe it now too."

"So you will free my wife?"

"We do not free terrorists!"

"I don't understand. What are you trying to say?"

"I think I've told you clearly, so you should understand that the fate of your future child depends on what testimony you intend to give at the hearing..."

"If I don't say what you want me to, what happens?"

"Nothing son. It's up to you what you choose to say. I only advise you, like I'd do for my own son, that you should confirm the monk was the organizer and..."

"What if I don't confirm it?"

"As I've already said nothing is going to happen. It'll still be proven that the monk was the leader of your criminal gang, but your testimony would be of additional help to us."

"What if I can't help you?"

"Then we can't help you either and I think you must understand, as it is, that a pregnant woman needs special care in prison."

"Yes, but they are fine, right?"

"So far they are, but you know what prison conditions are like. Things can happen any minute that might ..."

"That my wife may lose the baby?"

"I haven't said that, but you should know that no one will release a terrorist and a plane hijacker, even a pregnant woman."

"But the child has not done anything wrong, right? It isn't even born yet."

"That's what I'm telling you. Their fate depends on you."

"If my wife and child are going to be alright, I'll say anything the investigation and the court needs."

"That's because you are smart. Why should so many people sacrifice their lives for that scum of a monk?"

The pleased investigator continued, but Gega wasn't listening anymore. His mind was solely with the wall where he had to write two more words. He actually managed three: *mind the baby...*

Back in his cell, he thought about the investigator's words and how he would give the exact testimony demanded of him so it would save the baby. The main thing for him now was to hope the baby was born before the trial. Then, Gega could tell the truth, say everything. He could not confirm what they demanded of him since it was a lie: the monk was completely innocent and had not even been on the plane. This was why Gega would tell the truth. But he would do this only after his baby was born, with loud screams in one of the prison cells. It would be born like all babies are born, when their lungs fill with air for the first time.

Little did Gega know that those preparing to sentence him were far more cold-blooded than he could have ever imagined. No one could have imagined what lengths the authorities would go to, even in such a ruthless country ...

# THE VERDICT

The first unofficial verdict was passed before the trial and executed at night, only after the authorities finally became convinced that Gega would not publicly give the testimony that suited their interests.

For them, the problem of Tina's pregnancy was more important than Gega's testimony, since trying a pregnant woman could cause broad public compassion and pity towards the hijackers and the Soviet authorities really could not permit that. The Central Committee also considered that if the baby was born before the trial, it would cause additional problems for the government, so they quickly made the decision and carried it out that very night.

They did not wake up Tina. It did not matter to them whether the pregnant prisoner was awake or not because they had to give her something to make her sleep anyway. When Tina woke up, the people in white gowns paid no attention to her widened eyes, full of fear and question. Very quickly, in cold blood, they gave her a shot in the artery.

Tina immediately realized that these people were there for the evil deed she had often worried about. Every time she entertained such thoughts, she would get angry with herself for having such a bad opinion of people.

Yet, they really were not people, they were cold-blooded murderers, whose hearts and minds were not even slightly touched by Tina's desperate pleading not to kill the little unborn baby. Tina struggled until the end, until the last second, until she lost consciousness. She begged all of them, everyone in her cell that night, not to kill her child. But the drug they gave her was very strong and the murderers even looked at one another several times, surprised at how this young woman could struggle and resist for so long. In the end, Tina closed her eyes, drained of strength, defeated and asleep. She did not feel anything, could not see anything, when the several-month old fetus was cut out from her body.

The only thing that connected Tina with the world were the tears wetting her face. Tina cried. She was in a deep asleep and still cried...

There was probably no happier prisoner on earth than Gega when he was taken for interrogation. He felt like he was going on a date, and the most precious place for him in the whole world was that wall with Tina's words.

But that day there were no new words for him and he wondered if they stopped taking Tina for interrogations, or if she simply didn't have enough time to write even a single word. That day, he left only a question: *How's our little one?*

Several days later, when Gega was taken to interrogation again there was still nothing from her. Again, Gega thought there could have be many reasons for the lack of reply but he still felt a strange weakness in his knees and sweat at his temples.

Once in the interrogation room, Gega asked for water and began to think about what could possibly have happened.

At a loss, he decided to ask the investigator about Tina. He had no hope whatsoever of a truthful reply from the elderly investigator, but he had nothing to lose.

Gega drank some water and tried to act as calm as possible when he asked the investigator in a matter-of-fact tone.

"How is my wife?"

"Your wife is well."

"Are you also the investigator for my wife?"

"Your wife is interrogated by my colleagues."

"Then how do you know she's well?"

"I'm telling you what I know, son."

"Do you have any children?"

"I have good children."

"Unlike us? Have you ever written a letter to your sweet-heart?"

"I think I'm the one who asks the questions here."

"Sooner or later, you'll have to answer, too."

"Are you saying that to me?"

"To all of you."

"Are you threatening us?"

"I probably won't be able to anymore, but others will demand answers from all of you."

"For what?"

"For everything."

"First all of you will have to answer for what you have done. You have destroyed the lives of so many people and you don't even consider yourselves guilty."

"I have not killed anyone but I still consider myself guilty."

"And how is that expressed? You aren't helping the investigation, you will not name the others."

"I've told you already I'll say everything that's necessary if my wife and child are going to be alright. I've already testified about the monk too."

"And I've already told you that no one will let a plane hijacker and a terrorist go home, even a pregnant woman."

"I didn't ask you to do that. I agreed to give the testimony you wanted because I want my baby to be born, to stay alive, at least, if they're going to sentence me to death by firing squad."

"Don't be afraid, son, they won't sentence you to be executed. If you confess everything, don't be afraid of death."

"I'm not scared of the execution and death."

"Then what are you afraid of?"

"I'm afraid for my baby, I am afraid that it will be killed."

"It isn't born yet, how can it be killed?"

"Yes, but it will be born, and a baby born in prison needs so much care and attention."

"If it is born, they'll take care of it. Don't you worry about that."

"If it is born? What do you mean, if it is born?"

"Son, you understand that prison conditions are very bad for a pregnant woman."

"But you promised. I gave you the testimony. I wrote what you wanted me to."

"And it's very nice that you wrote it."

"But what if I change my testimony at the trial?"

"That doesn't matter. The main thing is the testimony that you have already given to the investigation. That's the way it is, according to Soviet laws."

"How?"

"You should have studied the laws first, son, and then hijacked the plane."

"But what about my baby?"

"As I said we cannot release a terrorist, even if it's a pregnant woman."

"But she can give birth here, in prison, right?" "She can, but..."

"But what?"

"But I've told you, and am telling you again, prison isn't the place for a pregnant women and she may have a miscarriage at any minute. If your wife intended to have a baby, she should have stayed at home."

The investigator said something else to Gega, but he wasn't listening anymore. His fist hit the investigator remorselessly, and he fell down with a thud. Gega didn't give him the chance to get up. He jumped on top of him, trying to strangle him with his bare hands.

"Fuck you! You promised they'd take care of the baby! Fuck you all! Murderers!"

Afterwards, in the cell, when Gega opened his eyes and wiped away the blood, he couldn't recall how those men who first hit him and then kicked him until he fainted appeared in the interrogation room so quickly.

When he regained consciousness, he could feel the taste of his own blood and tried to spit, but it proved to be quite hard, just like moving. He felt pain everywhere—his whole body was aching. He remembered the investigator's words:

"Don't leave any marks on his face, hit him low!"

He also remembered his utter surprise at how active the investigator was, who had been just been croaking and hardly breathing two minutes earlier. However, it was only a fleeting moment. He desperately wanted this horror to end but the it continued until they finally got tired...

After that day, Gega's interrogations abruptly finished. They no longer needed his testimony until the trial. Gega waited impatiently for the court hearing where he would see Tina. But he was also afraid of the meeting, afraid of facing the truth that Tina was not pregnant anymore. As long as hope still existed, a small sliver of hope, he did not want to face the truth.

He also knew he would see his mother at trial, who he had not seen or heard from since the hijacking. He would try to explain to her that he had not intended to leave her, that he had planned to take his mother with him later, take her away from this terrible country.

He also wanted to see his friends, who were together with him on the plane and who he had not heard anything about each other since their arrests.

He also thought of those friends who were not with him on that plane, but he suspected they had been interrogated as well, and he was right.

Others were also taken to interrogations, but the investigation was most of all interested in Irakli Charkviani, a close friend of Gega who was supposed to know more about the hijacking than the others. The Russian investigator, who had specially arrived from Moscow, initially thought that Gega had not asked Irakli to fly with them because Irakli's grandfather, Kandid Charkviani, was the former First Secretary of the Central Committee of the Communist Party of Georgia. However, having interrogated Irakli for the first time, he understood that the reason was completely different.

The strange young man surprised the Russian investigator from the beginning, as he insisted on answering his questions only in Georgian. Irakli was very calm as a baffled Georgian KGB employee translated his answers for the Russian investigator. The Georgian officer was genuinely surprised that Kandid Charkviani's grandson did not speak Russian, but the Russian investigator understood right away that Irakli knew Russian perfectly well (unlike the translator), as well as other languages.

The Russian investigator also understood that while talking to this strange young Georgian, he was talking to the new generation of Georgians; a generation that would never be obedient, conformist and submissive unlike their parents. Therefore, the Russian investigator was not surprised at Irakli's clearly anti-Soviet references in answers. Quite the contrary, it made the Russian investigator all the more eager to determine why he didn't go on the plane.

"Why didn't they want you to fly with them?"

"Who?"

"Gega at least, he was your closest friend, wasn't he?"

"Why *was*? Gega still *is* my closest friend."

"Sorry, I didn't mean that. I hope you won't think much about that."

"What did you mean?"

"I wanted to say that it isn't at all clear to me why Gega didn't tell you anything, especially since he knew you well. Sorry, knows you well."

"That's exactly why he didn't tell me anything, because he knows me all too well. He knew I'd refuse."

"But why? Are you trying to tell me you like the Soviet Union so much that you wouldn't betray it?"

"I believe I haven't expressed any sympathy towards Soviet authorities even once during our conversation, but I'm not a dissident either, and don't want to be."

"That's exactly what I'm interested in. What were the grounds for selecting the hijackers and were you, as Gega's closest friend, not among them?"

"I already told you, Gega knew I'd refuse."

"Why? You didn't want to fly?"

"I've always wanted to fly. I want to now as well and I'll fly. But not on a plane..."

The Russian investigator sat silent as he contemplated Irakli's answer, but he failed to grasp the young Georgian's meaning. So the investigator asked him the last question, only to break the awkward silence.

"What if you can't fly?"

"Then I'll swim across the sea."

"What?"

"The sea."

"How?"

"Singing."

"Are you joking?"

"I'm not joking."

"Shall we include that in the interrogation transcript just like that?"

"Yes, sir."

"How exactly?"

"Verbatim."

"How exactly?"

"I'll cross the sea swimming…"

After the interrogation, Irakli grew suspicious that Gega and the other hijackers would probably be sentenced to death and he shared his concerns with his friends as they were Gega's friends as well.

Most people in Tbilisi , and across Georgia, and across Georgia thought the hijackers would be spared death row. Their motivation was logical—the plane hijackers were not murderers, so shooting them would be excessive cruelty on the part of the authorities. Consequently, Irakli's friends met his theory with doubt. He himself wanted to know more, so he took advantage of his family connections. He found out the identity of the judge who was to decide on the main verdict at the upcoming trial and sought out his son. He met the judge's son at the university, after lectures, and told him directly what he wanted to know. The judge's son promised him to find out everything if, of course, he managed to extract it from his father. He was skeptical he would be successful.

That very evening the judge's son asked his father whether he was going to preside over the plane hijackers' trial.

"Who told you?" his father aggressively demanded.

"I was told."

"Who was it?"

"What difference does it make?"

"It makes a great deal of difference."

"Why?"

"It is practically a state secret. No one must know the identity of the judge until the trial itself."

"Well, your secrets are like our state itself. It's general knowledge you're to be appointed the judge of the case."

"Who told you?"

"What does it matter, they told me at the university, everyone knows it already."

"The university has always been an anti-Soviet nest."

"Well, they know it at the nest, already."

"I don't think this is something to joke about."

"I'm not joking with you either, and I seriously want to know what's going to happen."

"What do you mean, what is going to happen?"

"What will happen at the trial?"

"I'm not obliged to, and don't want to answer, especially because no one knows in advance what is going to happen at the trial."

"I'm not interested in details. I just want to know the verdict."

"No one knows what the verdict will be beforehand either and no one will be able to answer your question."

"Can you give me a simple answer to a simple question?"

"How?"

"Tell me: yes or no."

"What do you want to know?"

"Will they be sentenced to death?"

"I don't know, but plane hijackers, bandits and terrorists will be sentenced exactly as they deserve."

"Is that death by firing squad?"

"That's justice."

"That means they'll be executed?"

"I told you, I don't know..."

The son understood his father wouldn't tell him anything. He also understood that the verdict for the hijackers would be passed before the trial, if it wasn't passed already.

In the meantime, the judge, picked up the phone as soon as his son left the room.

"Hello sir, yes, it's me. When can you put me through? Yes, it is urgent. Yes, I'll wait."

The judge hung up the receiver and waited, without moving, for the phone to ring. He kept his eyes on the phone. With his index finger, he wiped a drop of sweat which dripped down his brow.

As soon as the telephone rang, the judge immediately picked up the receiver and sprang to his feet.

"Hello." He cleared his throat and continued. "I wanted to report to you that the information about my appointment has already leaked... How do I know? They have sent my son to find out about the verdict, asking whether they are going to be executed or not... What did I answer? What you and the Party have always been teaching us—that Soviet laws are humane, but that criminals must answer for their crimes and that the state will punish adequately those who have betrayed their homeland... Hello? Hello?"

The judge stood still for a long time, with the black telephone receiver pressed to his ear, though no one was listening to him anymore. The judge, of course, was replaced...

# EKA

The house search began at dawn on February 2nd 1984. Throughout the search, the father and daughter stood side by side, holding hands. The father said good-bye to her in such a way as not to scare Eka. Then Father Tevdore got to his feet with such composure, so much dignity, that no one dared to handcuff him. They followed him.

Several days after the arrest of the monk, they went to search his house again. The only person they found there was little Eka, who watched in astonishment as the men thoroughly searched the house. But Eka wasn't scared; she simply did not understand what else these unsmiling people could be looking for. She was still quite young, but not the little girl that Soso used to take for walks. Eka loved her dad's friends, but her dad was her real hero—the only monk who wore jeans, the most adorable dad on the face of the earth.

Little Eka stood motionlessly and waited for the unwelcome visitors to leave. She probably would not have moved at all had one of them not opened the cupboard where she kept her father's poems. He used to write these poems specially for her. When Eka was little she used to ask for bedtime stories, which her father gladly told, but sometimes she would also ask for poems, so her father made them up for her until she grew up. When Eka learned to write and went to school, she wrote down her father's poems, in large, round letters, in a notebook which a man was now leafing through. Then he closed it, opened it again and addressed his superior with a question:

"What do we do with this?"

"What is it?"

"Poems."

"Whose?"

"I don't know."

"Read them and you'll figure out. Ah, you won't be able to, so bring them along!"

The man was still looking at the poems and about to read them when he suddenly felt a terrible bite on his wrist and let the notebook go. Little Eka immediately picked it up, pressed it to her breast and began to move backwards, towards the wall.

The man first looked down at his bitten wrist in surprise, then looked at Eka closely.

"Your father is a terrorist," he spat out through his teeth. He started towards the child, but his superior understood right away that the notebook could not be taken away from Eka. He stopped his subordinate and asked him calmly.

"Were there only poems?"

"Dunno, there was nothing but poems, probably written by her."

"How could you tell, by the content?"

"What do I know about the content, the handwriting's childish."

"Have you finished already?"

The chief now looked at the others and without waiting for their answer, motioned all of them to leave the house. They obeyed.

Eka rushed to the window, moved the curtain aside and looked out. The strangers were getting into a car and she waited at the window for a little longer. When the car disappeared around the corner, Eka finally became convinced that the uninvited visitors had really left. She opened the drawer where she kept another book, a music notebook. The strangers could not have known that the monk, whose house they searched for weapons, wrote music as well. Eka wrapped up the sheets with her father's music together with his poems and tied them with a piece of string, and then she took a spade and went to the backyard. First she looked around to make sure no one was watching, and then began to dig. The hole she dug was not deep but the music and poetry were well hidden.

The cruelty of the authorities' propaganda was so vicious that nobody wanted to sit next to Eka after her father's arrest. She sat alone at her school desk like the daughter of a state enemy. She tried not to turn bitter. After the trial, the fourteen-year-old girl wrote a letter to the Party First Secretary, asking him to spare her dad. Realizing she would not get an answer, Eka went to the Central Committee in person. She attempted to get an answer everywhere she possibly could, everywhere she thought her dad would be.

For today's teenagers, it might seem utterly unbelievable that a little girl would undergo such pain to find her father. She spent several years going through distant camps—all on her own.

She was spurred on by unconditional love. She wrote about her love to her father in her letter, saying her life would lose its meaning without him. In the letter Eka also said she wasn't aware of the reason her parents had divorced, but she knew exactly why they had met in the old film studio courtyard. In those days Father Tevdore was Temur Chikhladze—a highly educated, green-eyed young man, very popular with girls. Temur fell in love with a woman who would later become Eka's mother.

At the time Temur fell in love, he was offered a part in a Georgian film *The Philatelist's Death* which was filmed in Sarpi, a Georgian-Turkish border village. Not surprisingly, the area was heavily guarded round the clock. As soon as he arrived to Sarpi, Temur sought out the most experienced fisherman and soon befriended a local to go out into the calm sea at night to fish.

Eventually, the border guards grew accustomed to the film crew—their eccentricities and nightly partying. And one night, when Temur borrowed the fisherman's boat, the guards did not suspect foul play—the boat and its owner were familiar they occasionally received the catch, which the young Russian guards happily accepted.

As he rowed away from the shore, Temur was surprised and expected to be stopped any minute. He awaited the guards with a small fishing rod in his hand, ready to provide evidence that he did not plan to violate the Soviet border and sail to Turkey.

Rather than breaking the waves, the boat floated in the calm sea. Close to dawn, Temur suddenly realized he was reaching the point of no return: he had to make up his mind whether he was to cross the line or return to his beautiful sweetheart. It was unclear how far the border guards would have allowed him to sail before springing into action but he eventually turned towards shore where Eka's future mother was waiting for him.

Years later, when the death sentence was announced for monk Tevdore Chikhladze, he addressed the authorities with only one request—he wanted to see his daughter Eka before the execution. However, the last will of this innocent man was turned down.

Even more years later, Eka wrote a book dedicated to her father—honouring him as a person who predicted the disintegration of the Soviet Union as long ago as her childhood. Eka's book included large amounts of previously unpublished, or completely unknown, material concerning the hijack case. She also focused on a theory that the authorities were warned about the planned hijack well in advance. The details of this argument were well grounded and persuasive as there were a lot of facts to support the idea. The authorities chose not to stop the implementation of the plan, as they needed the hijack attempt in order to organize their show-trial.

On the eve of the trial, the monk was interrogated for the last time. Several investigators and high-ranking officials were present. They wanted to know exactly what the monk would say at the trial, and wanted to be absolutely sure everything would follow their scenario. Consequently, when the monk once again confirmed that he would take the blame entirely upon himself in order to save the others, the investigators threw contented glances at the high-ranking officials. One of them addressed the monk.

"You must be ready for anything."

"I am ready."

"I don't believe you have understood me well."

"I am ready for anything if I am able to save them."

"For anything?"

"Yes, for anything. I am already thirty-three years old."

"We aren't here to find out your age. We're interested in several details and want to verify them."

"I'm listening."

"At the trial, you will admit that you led this terrorist group to plan to hijack the plane."

"At the trial I will admit that I was, and still am, the spiritual father of those who tried to take over the plane. That's why the main responsibility must be laid upon me."

"And are you ready to confirm, also in court, your role as the leader even if you know you'll be given a harsh sentence?"

"I'm ready for anything if I'm confident in saving their lives."

"In that case, you should know you may be sentenced to death. Are still not frightened?"

"No."

"Why?"

"Because I am a man of the Church and God will protect me. No one will protect them if they are sentenced to death."

"So, are you taking the whole responsibility and the highest penalty upon yourself, because you still hope to survive?"

"No, I haven't said that. What I mean is that since no one might be able to protect and save me, but only I can save them by doing this."

"But our opponents might still have some questions. Like why the person who planned everything didn't board the plane?"

"That's exactly why I deserve to be shot and not them. It was I who deceived them and sent the others to their destruction. I encouraged these young people while I hid in the monastery."

"Will you repeat this in court?"

"If only I am sentenced to death and save the others with my testimony, I'll confess to anything that you consider necessary"

"I think we have arranged all the details, but we still have some questions left."

"I have a question left too."

"Which is?"

"I'd like to know what their sentence will be."

"That depends on you, since the others may deny you masterminded the hijack."

"They'll probably do that, too."

"And in such case, what will you do, what will you say in court?"

"I'll say that they didn't tell me the exact date they were going and that they took another plane."

"You will tell a lie?"

"I've never told a lie and everything I'm telling you is the truth."

"Don't worry about that, we are less interested in the truth. The priority is that you say what's good for our case. For the purpose of state interests, even lying isn't a crime."

"But I really feel guilty, because I was their confessor and I should bear the responsibility."

"Don't worry about that either. You are going to bear the responsibility in full."

"I've told you, I'm ready for anything in exchange for saving their lives."

"We've already told you that their sentence depends on your testimony."

"I'll say everything as you prefer it, but they must be spared. They are still very young and they must live on." Long held back tears welled up in his eyes and the monk's voice trembled, but no one heard his last words. The investigators had left the room.

"Let's go back to the cell, Father," said the guard as the monk stood up.

When they were following the long, half-lit passage, the guard told the monk in a whisper, almost apologetically.

"I've read only half of it so far, Father, I'm a bit slow at reading."

"It's the kind of a book that you should read slowly."

"I'll give it back to you next week."

"You don't have to give it back."

"Don't you need it anymore?"

"Everyone needs that book."

"That means you need it too."

"I've got another one."

"Thank you, Father."

"Say thanks to the Lord."

"I want to say something to you too."

"Go on."

"You have never come out of the interrogation room so elated."

"Not elated. Pleased, probably. There's no joy around here."

"Does it exist at all?"

"Real joy exists elsewhere."

"Where?"

"In another world."

"Where?"

"When you read that book to the end, you'll understand everything."

"I already want to understand some things."

"And what is that?"

"The reason for your being pleased."

"The trial will be held soon and all of this will end."

"Is it going to end like you think it will?"

"The main thing is that it will end..."

# THE TRIAL

It was called the court of justice, but in reality there was no indication of justice. The hearing was scheduled nine months after the beginning of the investigation, though most of the witnesses were not even interrogated. Soviet law had no provision for the length of the investigation term, but it was clear that the authorities were in an extreme hurry to pass a verdict for the plane hijackers.

The trial began on August 1st, just when everyone is try to escape the scorching heat of the capital. The heat in the beginning of August in Tbilisi is notoriously so unbearable that even those sheltered in summerhouses close to the city flee to the sea in Western Georgia. Tbilisi would be empty, ensuring the authorities that it would be unlikely people would protest against the trial. Like a badly staged play, the government wanted a quick ending and made sure that only the parents of those on trial would attend the hearing.

Most of the audience in the courtroom was made up of KGB employees, and only the parents of the accused were permitted to attend. No one else, including former passengers of the hijacked plane, were there. Of the passengers allowed in, only those who would say exactly what the authorities wanted were selected. Despite this, none of these witnesses claimed that any of the accused were murderers.

Several days later, the verdict was scheduled. The night before, they summoned one of the passengers to meet with the KGB. He was quite an elderly man who, apart from his age, had been broken down by grief. His only son was in prison. He had been there for several years because of a traffic accident.

Though they gave him some water for his nerves, the man was so frightened and agitated he could not calm down until he was told the reason for his summons to the KGB. What they told him was probably worse than he expected. He only fully understood it the next day at the trial. He sat in the KGB official's room and nodded to the people in suits, while wondering why their ties were not choking them in such heat.

At the start, they were evasive.

"Your son's been in prison for the five year already."

"Yes."

"It must be very hard for you."

"It is."

"You probably want him to get out soon."

"Yes, I do."

"You might know that sometimes the prison term for some prisoners can be reduced and they can be released."

"Yes."

"You must be missing your son."

"I am."

"You probably know that only those prisoners who behave well are released."

"Yes."

"Or their parents."

"Yes."

"Or their parents behave well..."

"Yes."

"For instance, you can assist us, so that your son is freed from prison before his term is over."

"Yes."

"I hope you want to help your son."

"I do."

"But you don't know how."

"Yes."

"Yes you know, or yes you don't?"

"Yes."

"Yes what?"

The elderly man asked for more water, drained the glass, and asked for more. Only when he drank the second glass, was he able to utter what must have been the longest statement in his entire life:

"My wife used to write appeals for pardon. She still does. Everyone says it was the fault of the person, who is dead now, who crossed the street in the wrong place, but..."

"But nothing?"

"Nothing. He's in prison for a fifth year now."

"That's exactly what we've told you. Now you can help your son."

"What are you saying? They've asked for such a sum, that even if I sell my apartment, it still wouldn't be enough and..."

"Oh no no no, we aren't talking about money here. It's about assisting to the state in return for which the state will pardon your son."

"How can I assist you so that they let my son out of prison? What can an ordinary man like myself do?"

"It's exactly you who can do it, precisely because you're an ordinary, hardworking and honest man and your words will have decisive importance at tomorrow's trial."

"What are you saying? What can I say that's so important?"

"Say what you know and what you saw back then on that airplane."

"What could I see? I was lying on the floor the whole time."

"But you saw that they killed people, right?"

"Yes, I saw those who got killed."

"And?"

"And I have been sick ever since. My wife has been taking me to doctors ever since, but so far I don't feel any better."

"That's exactly what your assistance is going to be. You are to say the same thing tomorrow, at the trial, so that those who are guilty will be punished as they deserve. Is it fate that your innocent son should be in jail and those bandits live like heroes?"

"I've been thinking that as well. No one has ever said anything bad about my son and the investigator was saying the same, that it wasn't his fault."

"So, your son will come back home soon, while these terrorists receive a just punishment."

"Bless you if you do this kindness. Otherwise he won't be home in time to see mother, or myself, alive. We're both pretty finished waiting for him..."

"So, if tomorrow at the trial you tell the story of those murderers, in a couple of days your son will be at home."

"Why shouldn't I tell it? I'll tell everything in detail, what happened and how."

"Do you remember the faces of those who shot at the people?"

"How can I remember those shooting at us from the outside?"

"Forget them. You must recognize those who hijacked the plane and killed the people."

"How can I recognize them, I told you, we lay face down the whole time."

"It's not a problem to recognize them. They'll be sitting there in front of you, and when the judge asks you whether it was them, you will nod and confirm it. You do remember the faces of those who hijacked the plane, right?"

"How can I forget them?"

"So, it was them who killed the people and they should answer for it."

"If they killed them, don't you know that better than me?"

"The investigation has already determined everything, but an honest man like you, who was on that plane and can confirm it, will help both the state and his own son."

One official, who seemed to be higher in rank than the rest, saw the elderly man to the main entrance and sent him home in his office car.

"So, you know what to do tomorrow. We're counting on you." The KGB official said goodbye to him deferentially, firmly shaking the hand of his reliable witness.

The final day of the court hearing was scheduled for August 13th. The heat in Tbilisi was truly unbearable on that day and the government wanted the trial to be over as soon as possible, despite the fact that many details of the case were still completely unclear.

Over these thirteen days of the trial, the accused watched out for their parents and friends in the courtroom. Gega's mother Natela asked him with her eyes whether he was suffering from anything, because it seemed to her that her son was in pain. Gega replied with his eyes that nothing was bothering him, but Natela was certain something had happened in prison. She understood when her son was in pain. Gega also felt his mother was deeply worried but he could hardly hide his torment. From the very first day of the trial, he tried to be cheerful and smiled in order to conceal his pain. He was a very good actor, and he convinced those in attendance that he was alright—everyone except his mother.

Yet, it was ultimately a role Gega couldn't pull off. His anguish was more than he could bear. Tina wasn't pregnant—the fact became obvious to him on the very first day of the trial. But there was still a tiny hope that Tina had already given birth to their child, which would have explained her flat belly. He kept looking closely at her and Tina understood he was waiting for the answer directly from her. Hardly noticed by the others, Tina slightly shook her head. Gega immediately realized that everything was over.

In these thirteen days, the accused were given brief moments to exchange a few words with each other. During the breaks, Gega could have easily asked the tormenting question, and discovered how it all happened, but he chose not to hear the truth from his wife. He decided that hope was more vital now than the truth about their baby.

The final day of the trial began with the testimony of the monk, who addressed the judge, and everyone present at the trial, with regret.

"I was, and still am, the spiritual father of these people and that's why the whole responsibility for what they have done lies upon me. They are very young and can still rectify the mistakes they have committed. They can still be useful to society and our country. There have been enough victims, enough death. For these reasons, I ask you to show mercy towards them. If anyone is still thirsty for blood, consider me. I am the main culprit and let my punishment suffice to spare these young people."

The judge rudely interrupted the monk's speech and then someone called from the audience.

"What are you going to do if they spare you?"

"I've got an old map of Georgia at home. It's extremely detailed—with all the villages and churches across the country. I'll go searching for the remotest place and spend the rest of my life praying."

When the monk sat down, a grave silence hung in the courtroom for a long time, since he was the first person to mention the word "death" at the hearing. The silence was broken by the judge, who urgently summoned the elderly witness who had gone through a thorough briefing in the KGB building the previous night.

The judge respectfully addressed the witness and asked him to tell what he remembered. The elderly man spoke with sincerity:

"It was a bad thing, very bad. I'd been in hospital back then, here in Tbilisi, and when I felt a bit better, I was in a hurry to get back home. I'm angry at my wife even now, because it was her idea that I take the plane, not the bus, that it would be better for my health. Otherwise, planes aren't good at my age. I told her I'd take a train then, that it wouldn't be as bumpy as a bus, but she still said, no, take the plane, maybe you'll be back in time for the last tangerines, everyone has already picked theirs and the rest will rot. You know what women can be like when they start at you and ..."

"Please speak about the case."

"As for the case, I want to say that everything I've heard here is true. The only person I don't remember is that priest, but I do remember the rest on that plane. How could I forget? I wouldn't wish my enemy to have been there."

"So, you confirm that the accused are the same who were trying to hijack the plane?"

"I've told you, sir, that I remember them well, but I cannot recall that priest."

"So, you confirm that apart from the accused person you mentioned, you remember well the others, sitting there, to be the terrorists?"

"I remember all of them and I've told you, sir, that I can't recall the priest. One of them also had a beard, but he's not here and also, his beard was light, while this one has a black beard and that was a different one, he didn't look like this one…"

"I'm not asking you about the others. We are talking about the accused currently in front of you, present in the courtroom and whether you confirm that these are exactly the terrorists who attempted to hijack the plane on which you were one of the passengers."

"It was them, sir, I can't lie."

"Can you confirm that their armed attempt to hijack the plane caused fatalities?'

"Of course there were fatalities, both dead and wounded and some with broken arms and legs. When the plane started to fall down, the people were being mashed like…"

"Can you tell us which of the accused in particular were armed and with what types of weapons the hijackers shot at the passengers?"

"I don't know what they were holding, sir, I'm a peasant and don't know about such things, but when we landed and the troops were shooting at us from the outside with submachine-guns…"

"So, you confirm that the accused were armed?"

"Them? Of course, who has ever heard of a hijacking of a plane without weapons?"

"Can you tell us specifically whose shots were followed by the deaths, or bodily injuries, of any of the passengers?"

"How can I, sir? There was a lot of shooting and I was lying on the floor the whole time and didn't even lift my head up, while the shooting went on."

"And when the shooting stopped, you sat up, and probably saw the armed people—those now sitting in front of you."

"I sat up, but I couldn't stand up. I felt really bad and my mouth was very dry."

"And you probably saw one of them, with a weapon in his hand?"

"Yes, sir, I saw him and I remember well that it was him, because I'd seen him on TV, but I don't remember the name of that movie."

"Do you remember the weapon? What kind of a weapon did the terrorist have in his hand?"

"He had a bomb in one hand, sir, but not like in the war movies. He had a round bomb in one hand…"

"And in the other?"

"In the other? Should I say it, sir?"

"Yes, you must say everything that you know and remember, that is exactly why you are here."

"I don't know sir, if I say it, maybe I'll spoil something."

"It is vital for the investigation of the case and for the court that every detail is revealed."

"So, should I say it, sir?"

"Yes, please tell the court what the accused had in his other hand."

"He had a glass in the other hand."

"What glass?"

"It was an ordinary glass. He was bringing water for whoever felt bad."

The judge was caught unawares by the testimony. There was an unnaturally long pause before his next question.

"And then?"

"And then he brought some water for me too, and I felt a little better."

"And then?"

"What then, sir? If they die, that'll be a shame too…"

The voice of the elderly witness began to quiver, and then a tear rolled down his cheek and then he started loudly crying without restraint. The judge announced a break.

# THE END

It was no wonder that the elderly witness was not brought back after the break.

Although two people had mentioned death earlier that day, the severe verdict read out by the judge came as a shock not only for the accused and their parents, but even for the KGB officers present at the trial: Tina was sentenced to fourteen years in prison, the rest of them—to death by shooting.

Immediately after the verdict was announced, the accused were led out of the courtroom. Gega searched for his mother, who stood motionless. She only saw the back of her son as he was taken somewhere. She refused to believe it was true, that he would be executed.

None of Gega's friends believed it either, and they still believed there was a last chance to save them—a pardon that the government sometimes granted to death row convicts. It was now necessary to write a letter that would be

signed by the most reputable Georgians of the time. It had
to be addressed to the authorities with an appeal to spare
the lives of the young people who had gone astray. Several
people drafted the letter contained and secured the signatures, but they were not enough. They then began to search
for help from well-known and highly respected public fig-
ures all over Georgia.

Since it was the middle of August, most of them were
vacationing on the beaches of the Black Sea in Abkhazia.
Gega's friends and some volunteers combed the beaches
looking for sunbathing representatives of the Georgian
intelligentsia, beach by beach. They talked to them in whispers on the waterfront. Some intellectuals were motivated
to sign the appeal because they were deeply moved with
sympathy for Gega's fate. Others had to be secretly told that
the idea of the letter came from the government itself to
encourage their support.

The appeal for pardon was to be sent to Moscow, since
it was believed, sincerely and naively, that the decision to
sentence the hijackers to death had been taken in Moscow,
and that the local Georgian government only carried out
orders from Russia. In reality, everything was the other way
round. When Georgian authorities discovered that several
Georgian scientists, directors or actors who either coop-
erated with them, or were loyal to them, had signed the
appeal they were indignant. They worried about the reaction of Kremlin, who would undoubtedly be concerned that
the local intelligentsia was so openly and boldly defending
anti-Soviet individuals. It could be viewed in Moscow as a
sign that the government of Georgia did not have sufficient
control of its intelligentsia. The Georgian Central Committee Secretaries were incensed that a group they had given
apartments, cars and summerhouses would betray them
and sign a pardon without seeking approval.

After the verdict was passed on August 13th, a TV special entitled *The Bandits*, was aired ten days later. Over the ten days between the verdict and the inaugural broadcast, material from the trial was edited in such a way that the viewers would not have even the slightest doubt they were looking at hardened criminals, cynical murderers and bona fide terrorists who deserved to be executed.

There were, however, details that caused certain disagreement among the filmmakers. For instance, there was a necessity to include the Iverieli brothers' motivation for leaving the USSR. According to the investigation, their lifestyle was utterly immoral; full of sexual adventures and their real objective was to continue these exploits in the west. In truth, the brothers hoped to open their own clinic. This was not included in the film for fear it would not sound plausible and could antagonize the public.

The film also included other small details to illustrate the heartlessness of the hijackers. The group was accused of denying passengers the right to use the toilet on board the plane. In reality, the hijackers only appealed to passengers to remain seated when the plane was under heavy gunfire from the outside.

Several members of the intelligentsia, who had signed the pardon appeal, withdrew their signatures of support. Those who did not were summoned to the Central Committee and forced to withdraw support after threats and other methods of influence were issued. Some had to not only take back their signatures, but also write letters of explanation that apologized for the mistake they had committed against the government and the Communist Party. Yet, there were others who sacrificed their privileges and refused to revoke their signatures, maintaining their opinion that Gega and his friends should be pardoned. The wait for any pardon would be in vain. The authorities had made their decision.

Public opinion considered the decision so ruthless that they started to make up legends about Shevardnadze's cruelty. This was one of the only means of revenge for the Georgian public back then. There was a story about how Shevardnadze summoned Paata and Kakhaberber's father to talk about the death of his son. Whether the following story was true or not, it accurately reflects the pervasive public attitude at the time.

Paata's and Kakhaberber's father was a well-known Georgian physician and scientist who Shevardnadze knew personally. He was fired the day after his sons' arrest. Three weeks after the trial, he was summoned to see the First Secretary of the Central Committee.

Needless to say, Vazha Iverieli understood what, or more precisely who, the conversation would focus on. For the meeting, in the Central Committee of Georgia, where the fate of his sons was being decided, he deliberately chose to wear jeans. Vazha did not have a pair of his own, but found them in the boys' room. It was not an easy task to find them since his sons' room had been turned it upside down so many times during searches that the family gave up tidying it. After some time, he found the jeans, which smelled of his sons, put them on in front of a mirror and went to the Central Committee.

When a pass was given to him at the Central Committee, both low and high-ranking officials looked dumbfounded at the man who was going to meet with Shevardnadze wearing jeans—he was the first to show such daring.

Shevardnadze was looking down at his desk and did not hear the man's greeting on entering. What he certainly noticed was Vazha's jeans. Without raising his head, he pointed to a chair for the visitor to take and had a closer look at his jeans. He might have been angry and probably thought that this was a protest against the verdict passed on his children.

"You probably understand why I summoned you?"

"I don't know. I can only guess the talk will concern my sons."

"So, you do know."

"I am listening."

"No, I am listening to you."

"I have nothing to say to you."

"But you may have something to ask."

"What do you mean?"

"Your sons, of course."

"I cannot ask you anything for my sons."

"Why? You have no hopes for our mercy?"

"I have no right to ask you only for the life of my children. The others haven't done more wrong than my sons."

"So, you are asking me to change the verdict for all of them?"

"If that's why you have summoned me, then yes. But I cannot ask you to save only my boys, because I wouldn't be doing the right thing to others' parents, who don't know you in person and cannot come here, like myself, in order to save their children."

"The others have different circumstances."

"We are all in the same situation now."

"But they are about to lose one child each, while you are going to lose both, unless they are pardoned."

"Who is supposed to pardon them?"

"Moscow."

"Is there a chance?"

"We are doing everything in our power, but very often they make decisions and don't consult us. Had it been up to me, you know..."

"I know," said Vazha, despite the fact that he was not sure what this man would have done if the decision to change the verdict depended on him. Both were silent for a little while. Also, Vazha, did not tell Shevardnadze the truth, because there still was some hope to save his sons. It was Shevardnadze who broke the silence.

"There is a very little chance of altering the verdict for everyone, but I can manage to save one of your sons, at least. We have known each other for so many years and you have never asked me anything, until now..."

"I have not asked that, either."

"That's why I want to save at least one of the brothers. I've already talked to Moscow about it."

"How's that?"

"They'll probably change the verdict of the one who deserves his sentence to be changed."

Vazha got to his feet and was about to say something, but all of a sudden his throat went dry and he was unable to speak. Shevardnadze thought his guest wanted to thank him and made a gesture with his hand, as if to say "not at all." Vazha tried again to get the words out, but without any result, so he started slowly towards the door. When he opened the door, Shevardnadze stood up, approached Vazha and, almost in a whisper, casually asked him:

"By the way, which one do you prefer?"

Vazha understood that he would die, right then and there, if Shevardnadze said anything more to him, so he slammed the door hard behind him. Slammed the door and left.

Whether the story was fiction or not, the author remains unknown.

After her conviction, Tina was to be transferred to a women's penitentiary, while the others were to be moved to the dungeons of a very old prison in Ortachala where death row convicts were kept. There was only one night left in the KGB prison before the transfers were to be made. The monk approached the guard, who he had secretly given *St. John's*

*Gospel*, with his last wish:

"You won't see me anymore. They're moving me tomorrow."

"I know."

"To the death row."

"I know."

To wait for my execution."

"I know."

"Everyone should have their last wish fulfilled, right?"

"Tell me and I'll try to help."

"You know which cell Gega's in?"

"Yes."

"And Tina?"

"Yes, I know the girl's cell too."

"Can you let them see each other?"

"Tonight?"

"It's the last night here. They will never be able to see each other again. This is my last wish, too."

"The women's floor isn't my zone and I can't go in there without a key."

"Love opens all doors."

"When can we talk about that book, Father?"

"After you open the first door of love. It's right here, on the upper floor..."

"Are there many such doors waiting for me?"

"Many, but some of them you are going to open more easily."

"The first door is always more difficult, isn't it Father?"

"I've meant to ask you for a long time and I keep forgetting. How come you work here? It keeps surprising me and I keep forgetting to ask."

"I'll tell you that when I come back Father."

The guard looked at his watch, then smiled at the monk.

"I'll go upstairs now. It seems a good time, Father."

"It's always a good time, always," said the monk, more to himself.

He made the sign of the cross as the guard walked away. The guard consulted his wristwatch again and quickened his step. He strode down the passage, turned right, went up the stairs and noisily put *St. John's Gospel* on the table, in front of his superior, who had fallen asleep at the desk.

"What's this?" asked the superior as he looked at the cover.

"It's a book."

"I can see it's a book."

"I've confiscated it from a prisoner."

"Will prayers help them now? My grandfather was a deacon and what? Nothing. He spent his whole time praying in church and now he's lying in the churchyard, at the end of our village. I wish he'd lived long enough to see what a great man I have become. He'd only been to the city twice."

"Sir, I need the key to the upstairs toilet, I have to take a prisoner up there. His stomach's upset and his toilet is clogged. The plumber won't be in until tomorrow."

"Which prisoner?"

"I don't remember his last name, the one who's here because of the cannery case."

"Is he one of yours?"

"Yes, one of mine."

"What did you feed him, then?"

"His own canned food."

The superior laughed heartily and took out the key from his desk drawer.

"Hurry up. It's already midnight, and you know it's against the rules."

"But if something happens to him, they'll blame us and that'll be worse."

"You've become very smart lately. Are you aiming at my position, by any chance? Want to be the boss, boy?"

The guard laughed at the quip, but not as heartily as his superior, and continued on his way. He reached the end of the passage and went up the stairs to the upper floor. Then he turned left and began to count the cells. He stopped at the seventh on the right, looked back first, into the half-lit passage, then knocked on the door with the key. He didn't wait for the answer, unlocked and unbolted the door. Gega was standing in the cell.

"Come out, quick," the guard whispered.

"What's going on?"

"I am doing a favour for the monk. His last request."

Gega and the guard quickly passed the corridor, turned right and ascended the stairs. The upper floor security, utterly amazed, asked where he was taking the prisoner at such late hour.

"His wife's in number 19. Only five minutes and I'll take him back again."

"You realize what punishment you're going to get for this?"

"If they don't see each other now, they never will. He got a death sentence today and is being transferred to death row."

"If he is, you might get his cell starting tomorrow."

"You refused to give me the key and I took it by force. That's what you can report if they ask for an explanation."

He snatched the cell key from the guard on duty and went down the corridor with Gega. Gega was more surprised than the guard on duty.

"You know, I didn't go to see the monk, even once," he whispered.

"When?"

"Before I was arrested. He kept waiting for me..."

"It's here," said the guard, stopping at cell 19. He knocked quietly, turned the key, opened the door and let Gega inside.

Tina was sitting on the bed, barefoot, wearing a white chemise. The bed was at the wall facing the door. The cell had a small, heavily barred window with another, faded brick wall beyond it.

Tina sat on the bed without saying anything. She only listened to Gega as he sat next to her. He carefully, very carefully, stroked Tina's fingers.

"Don't worry about it… My granddad was also sentenced to death, but he survived. My other granddad, who I'm named after, was also 23 when he was sentenced to death, and he told Lavrentiy Beria while speaking Mingrelian: *"I'm not afraid of death, you'll follow me there and we can talk then."* They brought him out of the Metekhi prison, at night, made him stand with his back to the river. My granddad asked them not to shoot him in the back, as he preferred to look death into the eyes. And so they aimed at him directly, shot and missed on purpose, because they had Beria's had orders to do so. As I was told, my granddad used to say afterwards that Beria did something much worse to him than death by keeping him alive… He's still alive, you probably remember him—at our wedding he was kissing you on the forehead all the time and crying… They won't shoot me either, don't worry, something will finally happen and they won't shoot me …"

There was a timid knock on the door and Gega stood up.

"I'm coming," he said in a very low voice.

He sat down again, strongly clasped Tina's fingers, which he had missed so much, with his right hand. Then he started to cry.

Then, before the guard locked the door, Gega threw a final glance at Tina still sitting on the bed. Her face seemed to glow and that was how Gega would remembered her forever– sitting on the cell bed, barefoot with wet eyes…

# THE FLIGHT

Despite everything, a majority of the public refused to believe the men on death row would be executed. Such wishful thinking caused some to invent various alternative scenarios and the most widespread one involved Siberia. It was said, that as a rule, death row convicts were not executed but sent to secret Siberian work camps instead. It was believed the same fate awaited the airplane hijackers. In reality, the authorities followed through with the execution. However, it did take some time after the verdict, as they had to wait for approval from Moscow to proceed. The procedure was customarily delayed for as long as several years. In this case, they were executed a month and a half after the sentence was passed, on October 3rd.

There was no official announcement, and no notification to the parents and families, at the time or afterwards. Information about Gega and his friends' execution still managed to spread across the country. It's worth remembering that

western radio channels were the only source of alternative information under the Soviet regime. Many Georgians
found out the news and heard about everything the Soviet
authorities thoroughly concealed only by means of these
*enemy voices*, as they were referred to in the official media.
The distressing information about the plane hijackers was
broadcast by *Voice Of America* the very day they were executed, but most people refused to believe that it was true
and held out hope.

As if to further add to the misery, Gega's grandfather,
who had miraculously escaped death in the 1930s at the
same age as Gega, died on the exact same day…

The cells of the death row convicts were in the dungeons
of the Ortachala prison, on the very last underground level.
The prisoners were taken to be shot into a special room,
on the same floor. However, it was not only the death row
convicts on this floor. Other inmates were on this level, and
knew very well who was in which cell and who was transferred where and when. Needless to say, some inmates had
more info than the others. Dima Lortkipanidze, one of the
notorious criminals, was kept one level above. He was born
in Paris, in the family of Georgian political emigrants, so
his anti-Soviet views were not fleeting. Several women prisoners arrested for illegal trade were kept next to Dima's
cell, waiting to be transferred to the women's penitentiary.
They used to hum and sing, which roused Dima's interest, so once he questioned the warden about the humming
inmates. The warden complained about their singing as
he was severely reprimanded for the poor discipline on his
floor. He was also surprised that these women, mainly shop
assistants and accountants, were so good at singing. Dima
motioned the warden to come closer and asked him in a
lower voice:

"If they sing loudly, will they be heard down there?"

"Down where?"

"On death row."

"With cells locked, how will they?"

"But they can be heard in the corridor?"

"Well, if they sing at the top of their voices, they'll probably be heard."

"Probably or for sure?"

"Probably."

"So listen. Do me a small favour and you'll be rewarded."

"Just don't make me lose my job ..."

"Yeah, you've really got a job that would be a shame to lose. So listen carefully."

"I'm all ears."

"Down there, on the death row, there's a guy, Gega, an actor."

"Yes, I know, that airplane business. The others are down there too."

"We can't help the others, but Gega needs help. He's quite young."

"I know, I've seen him in the movies, but ..."

"So, you like movies too. Now tell me, when will Gega be taken to be executed? How soon will you know about it?"

"Right away, the warden on that floor is my cousin."

"The moment they take him out, I need to know straight-away."

"Please don't make me lose my job, I've got two small children. If I could at least know what you're going to do..."

"Nothing special. When Gega's taken to be executed, you must tell the women to start singing, as loud as possible. Tell them it's my request to hearten Gega. Tell them he's taken to be shot."

The warden stood in amazement and listened to this strange prisoner so utterly unlike anyone he had ever seen in his career...

They were all executed on the same day. Special effort was made to stop the news from spreading and in most cases it worked. The monk and the brothers were taken out of their cells at daytime. They opened the door to Gega's cell and he met them standing tall, still believing it would not happen. He had no idea where he was being taken; did not know there was a room at the end of the passage, where his final sentence awaited him. On the way, Gega heard distant singing, from somewhere above, but thought he was imagining it. He smiled slightly, very slightly. One floor above, the women prisoners sang earnestly, standing very close to the locked window of their cell, singing loudly and crying. Unlike Gega, Dima Lortkipanidze could hear them very well. He was shouting Gega's name and banging his fists on the cell door until they were raw and covered in blood.

Dima's voice carried through the entire prison. Within seconds, other inmates joined him and soon every-one in the Ortachala prison knew that down in the cellar, a man was about to be executed. Within seconds, all prison floors were echoing Gega's name until their voices were hoarse. When Gega reached the end of the corridor, the rumble became so intense that the wardens accompanying him looked deeply worried. It might have been due to haste, or the Soviet Empire was really was rotting, because as soon as Gega stepped into the room, the waiting executioner shot him from behind, in full accordance with his instructions. But his gun misfired. The unexpected snag threw the executioner into a state of panic. With a mysterious calm, Gega turned to his executioner with a smile.

"Earlier you could at least kill people, now you can't even do that anymore."

The killer fired for the second time and suddenly everything was over...

Although the parents of the dead hijackers were not notified of the execution, the Soviet authorities had some rules that were even more ruthless. After October 3rd, the families were sent bills, and they were obliged to pay the cost of the bullets used for killing their children. Each bullet cost three roubles, but Gega's mother had to pay six—with the extra for the first jammed bullet.

The executioners were paid fourteen roubles for each executed prisoner on top of their monthly salary. What does it say about a society where the price of human life cost fourteen roubles?

They were not heroes. What they did is considered a crime everywhere.

Their parents, families, and friends never claimed they were innocent. They always believed they should be made to answer for what they did. Hijacking was a crime anywhere, especially when it involved fatalities, and the group had to be punished.

Yet, there was also a firm belief that that the state's extraordinary brutality and eventual murder of the hijackers was a crime arguably worse than the hijacking itself. A monk, who did not even participate in the actual hijacking was persecuted and condemned for a crime he played no part in.

The impression he left, however, was long lasting. His guard in Tblisi's KGB prison quit his job and eventually went to find the monk's remote monastery. A legend of the famous monk was instantly born in the local village. Many believed that he survived his execution, and that an innocent man was spared.

Even today, many people in Georgia believe the airplane hijackers are still alive in some far off place. They desperately wanted to fly away and they did…